Tokyo Nights

a novel by
Donald Richie

Introduction by David Cozy

Photographs by Isaac Diggs

Printed Matter Press

Tokyo Nights

Copyright © 2005
Donald Richie
All rights reserved

Originally published: London, Olive Press, 1988
First revised edition: Tokyo, Tuttle Publishing, 1994
Second revised edition: Tokyo, Printed Matter Press, 2005

Tokyo Nights: Introduction
Copyright © 2005
David Cozy

Tokyo Nights: Illustrations
Copyright © 2005
Isaac Diggs

The pictures in this book appear in the size requested by the photographer and approved by both author and publisher.

Layout & Design by Studio Z

Printed Matter Press
Yagi Bldg. 4F, 2-10-13 Shitaya, Taito-ku,
Tokyo, Japan 110-0004

E-mail: info@printedmatterpress.com
http://www@printedmatterpress.com

In association with Wandering Minds International

Printed in Japan

ISBN 1-933606-00-2

for Christopher Isherwood

HIPPOLYTA: But all the story of the night told over,
And all their minds transfigur'd so together
More witnesseth than fancy's images,
And grows to something of great constancy
But, howsoever strange and admirable.

A Midsummer-Night's Dream
Act V, Scene I

Introduction

Donald Richie is a modernist. So clear is that upon reading this new edition of Tokyo Nights that one wonders why so few have noticed. Perhaps it is that modernism is considered by many to be a dead letter. The conventional wisdom seems to be that it thrived in the early days of the last century, but has now joined Pre-Raphaelism and Futurism in the museum of dead literary and artistic movements. As Richie, born in 1924, is still writing and publishing in the twenty-first century, he couldn't be a modernist. He must be something else - a post-modernist, perhaps?

In addition to being of the wrong time to be a modernist Richie is also in the wrong place. Japan has been his home for more than five decades, and it has also been his subject; he has written widely and brilliantly on aspects of Japanese life ranging from film to gardens to fashion to tattoos. Studying the reaction to this tremendous body of work one sees, however, that Japan has, for many readers, been a sort of fun-house mirror which distorts Richie's achievement. Because Richie has written so extensively about Japan it has become almost impossible for his readers to see him as other than a Japanologist concerned simply with conveying information about the place. The rising sun has obscured the fact that Richie is an artist who in the best of his work has endeavored to mold the facts of Japan into patterns that are aesthetically satisfying - to do, that is, just what the canonical modernists did for Dublin, London, Berlin, and elsewhere. James Joyce said of *Ulysses*: "I can justify every word," and one feels certain that Richie could say the same of this spare little gem, *Tokyo Nights*.

This passion for order, for the creation of art in which there is nothing gratuitous, in which every fragment is there in the service of the overall formal integrity of the work, is one chracteristic of modernism, and this tendency arose, in part, in response to the increasingly chaotic state of the world in the early twentieth century, a time when the old certainties were breaking down. Whether one believes, with Virginia Woolf, that it was "on or about December 1910 [that] human nature changed . . ." or with D.H. Lawrence that "it was in 1915 that the old world ended," or with Richard Ellmann that "1900 is [a] . . . more convenient and accurate [date]," there can be little doubt that the world and people's ways of understanding it were no longer what they had been. Indeed, so momentous were these shifts that it is hardly excessive to say, as did Charles Péguy in 1913, that "the world has changed less since the time of Jesus Christ than it has in the past thirty years."

Among the most important forces behind the chaos that gave birth to modernism is the rapid advance of science and technology which occurred in the late nineteenth and early twentieth centuries. Consider, for example, that, as Robert Hughes has noted:

> The first twenty-five years of the life of the archetypal modern artist, Pablo Picasso - who was born in 1881 - witnessed the foundation of twentieth-century technology for peace and war alike: the recoil-operated machine gun (1882), the first synthetic fibre (1883), the Parsons turbine (1884), coated photographic paper (1885), the Tesla electric motor, the Kodak box camera and the Dunlop pneumatic tyre (1888), cordite (1889), the Diesel engine (1892), the Ford car (1893), the cinematograph and the gramophone disc (1894). In 1895, Roentgen discovered X-rays, Marconi invented radio telegraphy, the Lumière brothers developed the movie camera, the Russian Konstantin Tsiolkovsky first enunciated the principle of the rocket drive, and Freud published

fundamental studies on hysteria. And so it went: the discovery of radium, the magnetic recording of sound, the first voice radio transmissions, the Wright brothers' first powered flight (1903) and the annus mirabilis of theoretical physics, 1905, in which Albert Einstein formulated the Special Theory of Relativity, the photon theory of light, and ushered in the nuclear age with the climactic formula of his law of mass-energy equivalence, $E=mc2$.

To read Hughes's list is to understand the profundity of the change which was taking place, and to understand that the modernism which flourished in all the arts was a response to the cataclysm of the times. If the cataclysm had ended in, say, the year of Richie's birth, or in the mid-1940s when he arrived in Japan, we might then believe that modernism had done its work and could now be stuffed and mounted. One need only glance at the papers, glance at the internet, glance around one, to see, however, that the cataclysm is not just ongoing but accelerating. The concerns and methods of the modernists remain, therefore, as relevant as ever. Sensing as we do that the chaos of the times may have got the better of us, we hesitate now to describe artists as "mastering" their subjects, but we still crave the delight that aesthetic mastery can bring. Thus, at a time when many of our most advanced literary artists feel that it is sufficient to mirror the world's chaos, one welcomes a novel such a *Tokyo Nights*, a novel which doesn't just capture the chaos of Tokyo nightlife in the bubble years of the 1980s, but arranges that chaos into a pattern aesthetically pleasing and coherent.

The greatest of latter-day modernists, the late Guy Davenport, has written that "abstractions are mud pies." With that dictum in mind let us leave behind the mud pies and look instead more closely at what Richie, in *Tokyo Nights*, has given us and what it is that makes this work modernist.

Foremost among examples of Richie's modernism is his willingness to dispense with naturalism. Though he certainly gets the details of mid-80s Tokyo life right, these details remind one of the "real" (recognizable) eye and nose in Picasso's aggressively Cubist *Portrait of D.H. Kahnweiler*, or the real (no quotation marks necessary) bit of newspaper pasted into his *Guitar, journal, verre et bouteille*. Within a pattern of events and settings which does not in any literal way mirror reality, the details Richie pastes in - bars in which "Bruce Springsteen followed Grieg and was followed by Shep Fields and his Rippling Rhythm," cafés which feature Kraft on Ritz, nightspots in which the hostess can never quite get her gown zipped up - act as signposts guiding us through the fantasy Richie spins. (And Kraft on Ritz, Springsteen mixed with Grieg, will be no less exotic for many readers than the tokens of Parisian café life which feature so prominently in the Cubists' work.)

These bits of reality also help to ensure that Richie's work, in the best modernist style, never descends into facile surrealism. Richie's novel is a fantasy not in the manner of Dali's drooping watches but rather in the manner of Shakespeare's *A Midsummer Night's Dream,* the text which undergirds *Tokyo Nights* somewhat in the manner that the *Odyssey* undergirds Joyce's *Ulysses.* As in *A Midsummer Night's Dream*, Richie's tale begins as the sun goes down, but where Shakespeare's lovers have their adventures and misadventures over the course of a single night, Richie's are mixed up for an entire season of nights, from early summer to late fall. Each chapter advances us further into the deepening darkness,.

The progression through the seasons, through the chapters, has the inevitability of, say, Bach's progression through the keys in the *Goldberg Variations.* As in a set of musical variations each of Richie's chapters is linked to those which precede it and those which follow it by elements which, often in altered form, recur. In *Tokyo Nights* the setting is, as it were, the ground bass. Each of the chapters takes place at night in a bar, café, or restaurant of one sort or another. We move from a hostess-bar called the Yamato to a host-bar called The Empire to a lesbian-bar called Elle to a disco called Titania and so on through the nights. Within each of these settings - over this ground bass - we get the play of melodies in different arrangements, the six characters, three men and three women who, in varying combinations and moving toward different ends, disport themselves through the Tokyo nights.

Joyce, Picasso, and Bach have each been invoked to illustrate facets of *Tokyo Nights*. The first two are unavoidable in any discussion of modernism, and the work of the last sets the standard for the sort of structural integrity which characterizes Richie's novel. To compare Richie's work to that of these titans, however, is to suggest that it has a similar weight. It does not, and for that we must be grateful. *Tokyo Nights* is a comedy of manners and the last thing such a comedy should be is weighty. Neither will one find deep psychologies to probe in any of Richie's characters. They are types, and that is entirely appropriate to the sort of work Richie has given us.

(One notes, however, that when, here and there

in the novel, the geometry of the narrative leaves the actors alone, they can show flashes of humanity all the more moving for being out of character - the very thin character they had hitherto been allowed. See, for example, the final chapter of the farce in which Richie's characters, like Shakespeare's at the end of *A Midsummer Night's Dream*, "wake up.")

Richie's modernism, it becomes clear, derives not from heavyweights like Joyce (much less Musil or Broch) but rather from that lighter strand of modernism which one is tempted to characterize as English: the work of Ronald Firbank, Ivy Compton-Burnett, and most importantly, the Henry Green of *Party Going* - the 1939 novel Green wrote in response to Edward Garnett's request that he produce "something amusing." Richie acknowledges his debt to this novel, also a comedy of manners in which a great deal of space is devoted to the relations of shuffled and reshuffled combinations of characters, by embeddng an exact quote from *Party Going* in the final pages of *Tokyo Nights*.

It is not only the matter or the lightness with which that matter is treated that Richie's book has in common with Green's. There is also a stylistic link. In each case the author employs an English which owes something - in Green's case indirectly, in Richie's directly - to another language. The language which colors Green's English is Arabic, or at least the Arabic-inflected English of Charles Doughty's *Travels in Arabia Deserta*. Doughty's attempt to render the abrupt juxtaposition of spoken Arabic into English resulted in a distinctive prose style which eschewed what Green called "an elegance too easy," an easy elegance he wished to avoid. In Richie's case, as he explained in an introductory note to the first edition of this novel, "one of the conventions of [*Tokyo Nights*] is that English is Japanese."

Green knew no Arabic. Richie, on the other hand, does know Japanese, and is thus able to have his characters employ, in the English we are reading, the conventions of spoken Japanese in a manner that is entirely convincing. The neglect of pronouns in Japanese and the inherent vagueness of the language as it is commonly spoken has, for example, obvious comic potential - are we talking about a new shower system or actor Ken Takakura's penis? - which Richie exploits to the full. These linguistic importations, though, are more than mere hijinks employed for comic effect. Certain aspects of Japanese speech, for example, such as the stock phrases which characters repeat throughout *Tokyo Nights* (as Japanese people repeat stock phrases throughout their lives) support the novel's musical structure, repetition being integral to music. Richie's importations of Japanese conventions into English, therefore, are essential components of the novel's structure and thus, it becomes clear, part of an endeavor Richie is making to be true to the exhortation of another canonical modernist, Ezra Pound. Richie, in *Tokyo Nights,* makes it new.

Pound wrote a poem which reads in its entirety:

The apparition of these faces in the crowd;

Petals on a wet, black bough

He called for poetry with "fewer painted adjectives impeding the shock and stroke of it," and would surely have applauded another aspect of Richie's attempt to make it new, his willingness to expunge from his narrative everything that is inessential both at the level of the sentence (no unnecessary adjectives or adverbs) and of event (no unnecessary linking scenes, indeed no linking scenes at all, between any of the Tokyo nights). Just as Pound could have inserted, between the two lines of his poem, an account of the person who sees the faces and an explanation of that observer's awe, so Richie could have inserted, between his Tokyo nights, accounts of his characters' Tokyo days. How much more powerful, though, is Pound's poem without extraneous explanation, and how much more powerful are Richie's snapshots presented with nothing between them to impede the (gentle) shock and stroke of his tale.

One can extend the strand of modernism to which Richie's *Tokyo Nights* belongs backward through Green, Firbank, and Compton-Burnett, all the way to Oscar Wilde, but extending it forward is more difficult. Modernism as a whole, sometimes under the alias "post-modernism," will live as long as we need art to make sense of the booming and buzzing chaos within which we live, but, with the possible exception of Muriel Spark's work, the strain of modernism to which Richie's novel belongs, this particular way of making it new, is, it appears, on the brink of extinction. Spark is eighty-seven years old. Richie is eighty-one, and his most recent novel, *The Memoirs of the Warrior Kumagai,* derives from an entirely different tradition than *Tokyo Nights.* The pleasure which readers will find in *Tokyo Nights* is, therefore, tinged with regret. The strand of literary modernism it represents is not the most important one, but discerning readers can only lament its impending end.

David Cozy

February, 2005
Tokyo

Tokyo Nights

1

Bong went the clock and the Ginza flowed, six on a payday Friday night, late spring, the sun just going down. The big Hattori clock went pink in its tower and Mitsukoshi glowed; a rooftop Shinto shrine gleamed once in the sinking sun and down below the sidewalks surged. The light went green, stopped taxis revved, bikes roared and, squat before fancy Wako, the phone-board pachinko-like lit up. Another bong, the last, and walkers ebbed like surf as buses, trucks, the family car, filled the street, red all ahead. One cordovaned foot now safely on the curb, Hiroshi Watanabe heard the final stroke, cast an eye to the high clock, dodged a Honda, checked his Seiko, rounded the Burger King, skirted the Dairy Queen, ran right past the Cozy Corner, and down an alley hung with bar signs far as the eye could see; then into a side street, sky pale, sun gone as the bar signs flicked on, then in and under an old-fashioned kamban upon which was carved Yamato - the name of Old Japan.

He ran down the stairs, past the fake Fabergé in its fancy nook, the real Louis Seize commode reflecting in the foyer, and into the club itself empty but for its near-Empire chairs, tambour tables, pouffes, a love-seat, shelf upon shelf of Johnny Walker Black, four golf trophies, two stuffed fish - gifts of customers - a crystal chandelier and, under it, Mariko Matsushita showing impatience.

- So you're finally here, she cried.

- I hurried. Traffic. Payday.

- Well, Just catch your breath. Then: Payday. Don't I just know. Cleaned out. These girls.

She glared at a closed back door behind which was the kitchen and, presumably, the girls.

- Who's for him? he wondered.

- A new one, I thought. Pretty. In a way. The way foreigners seem to like.

Hiroshi's client (and friend, he often said) was due that evening back in Tokyo once more, buying it was hoped, selling it was feared. And Mariko, madame and sole proprietor of the popular Yamato, was to have (Hiroshi paying) a small and intimate repast.

- Seeing all that one is doing, one would have thought one could have come bit early. And a for-eigner as well. So upsetting.

- I am a bit early. I am an hour early.

- It is so difficult, having to do everything by one-self. Is it raining out?

- No. It is a beautiful spring evening. Why did you think it would be raining?

- Spite. Everything else has gone wrong.

She then put on a large and sorrowful face and told why. The cuisinart had broken, so no miso soup. Then three - three! - of the girls had called in sick (colds, though one a miscarriage for sure.) And then she got the estimate for the remodeling of the Yamato. Just a little Spanish colonial, she'd thought - and, oh, Watanabe-san, I cannot tell you! Tears. Here he responded with practiced pats and she raised mascaraed eyes.

This was apparently why she had wanted his earlier arrival, so that he might hear particularly of the financial woes. Had one thought that perhaps there was more here than just owner and patron one would have been correct.

As though in proof she suddenly and accusingly said: You're putting on weight again. It doesn't become you.

- Sorry, I'm sure, he said with a smile.

- Older men have to take care, was the reply.

He was careful to say nothing of older women and, after more smiles and assurances, she was soon wearing that smile clients called adorable.

At that point he said: But, you must remember, my dear, that I am busy as well.

Thus they occupied themselves until it was seven, after which the girls, all in their evening finery, were lined up and given their customary pep talk by Madame Mariko.

- All right, girls, I want you to give your all for old Yamato; keep up the spirit; make ours the winning team, etc.

Then the Yamato was declared open.

While awaiting the foreign guest they were joined by the new girl. She was introduced as Mitsuko Koyama and, when Mariko was called away by Midori's jammed zipper, offered that she was just eighteen and that this was her first time.

- You will like my friend. He is foreign.
- How foreign?
- American.

This she considered, then her brow cleared as though relieved at thought of the familiar. But then again the forehead creased: I don't have any languages.

Hiroshi smiled. Never fear. He likes Japan very much. He understands us. Why, he understands us better than we understand ourselves. And he speaks Japanese. He speaks just like we Japanese. He speaks that well.

- Who speak well? asked a voice and there stood the foreigner himself, a smiling individual who was introduced as Mr. Paul.

Mitsuko announced herself honored and answered his bow with one pert, outstretched hand. Then Mariko, returning from the kitchen, gave a small cry of welcome and tripped over to embrace Hiroshi's old friend.

- Welcome, welcome, she cried. Such an old friend. And, to Mitsuko: He understands us so well. He understands us better than we understand ourselves. Do sit down.

Over the Chivas Regal, the Camus Napoleon, the Jack Daniels, the Wild Turkey, the Old Crow and the single Bireley's Orange (for our Mitsuko here) they spoke more of the smiling, honored guest in their midst.

- He just loves old Japanese things, said Mariko, addressing the girl. The older the better. He even likes our tansu chests. Isn't that sweet? Of course, he's never had to live with them. Still, one can't but be touched. All that distance, just to come here and take an interest in our old things.

This was met with smiles and complacency. Then they went on to speak of the weather, of the beauty of the spring sunset, of the coming rainy season and of the trade imbalance.

After this last, Mariko went to check on Midori's zipper and Hiroshi, perhaps on behalf of his smiling foreign friend, turned the talk toward little 'Miss' Mitsuko here.

- Oh, you live in Tokyo, then? Ah, with your mother, I presume. How dutiful. Then: She-lives-with-her-mother. This to Mr. Paul.

- Does she know you're working in a place like this? then asked Hiroshi with a sly smile, in answer to which Miss Mitsuko properly looked down at her folded hands, her lap, the floor.

- Not that it is not perfectly respectable, he added with a firmish nod. Still - a pretty girl like you with all these men.

And he turned to look at Mr. Paul, the only other man in the place.

This was as far as he got before Mariko returned, burdened with raisin butter, caviar, sembei, and Kraft on Ritz.

- Please, said Mariko with a large gesture. It is nothing at all but help yourselves.

- She's good to her mother, said Paul, mouth full.

Mariko turned to Hiroshi and wrinkled her nose: Isn't it sweet to see people get on together? Even though he is foreign and all.

- But me, she continued, sigh, sipping the Chivas, biting a Ritz, I am just too old-fashioned for such modern ways. Just a daughter of Old Japan, you might call me.

Having said this, she suddenly sat straight and addressed Hiroshi: I have just had this wonderful idea! Why not do the Yamato all Japanese! Think of it! The novelty! The sensation!

Hiroshi looked around, perhaps remembering how much that chandelier had cost, how much the

Limoges panels on the kitchen door, how much the portrait of Marie Antoinette in the *dames*. Perhaps also thinking of how much fusuma and shoji and tatami would cost now that no one was using them anymore, now that the unit price had soared.

So: I don't know about that. Seems a bit old fashioned.

- No, no, no, cried Mariko. Don't you see? it has gone beyond that. It is so old-fashioned that it is fashionable again.

She further exclaimed that with foreign things so rife what more titillating than tradition? Things gone so far that Old Japan was like a foreign land - and what further novelty than that?

But her observations and his objections were silenced by the floor show, performed for just the four of them, and for Midori in the corner fussing with her zipper. It consisted of a young person in harem outfit, with veil, rotating her stomach.

Mariko, noticing Hiroshi's visible appreciation, pinched him, then turned to Mitsuko and, above 'Anitra's Dance', said: Left over from the last remodeling. It was all Arab, you see. To get the oil sheiks. None came, though. That's when we went French.

Mitsuko nodded and stared: Very educational, a belly dance.

- *Danse du ventre*, corrected Mariko. Then: It was quite nice. We had *Shéhérazade* on all the time.

Bernstein's. Until it got this click.

Hiroshi, still rubbing where he had been pinched, turned to Paul, indicated the rotating female and said: Nice little girl. Talented. From Saitama. Went to school especially to learn.

Mr. Paul nodded, appreciative, and Mitsuko, prodded, took his hand.

Removing her finger from the girl's back, Mariko pulled Hiroshi's sleeve and glanced meaningfully down at the clasped fingers. She beamed and he responded with a bleak smile, then all hands were joined in applause.

After which: Seems a slow night, said Hiroshi looking at the empty tables.

- Have some caviar. Iranian, invited Mariko. My crowd gets later all the time, especially on paydays for some reason. Isn't she sweet? This to Mr. Paul who nodded, his mouth full. Like real lovebirds. This to Hiroshi-san.

Bruce Springsteen followed Grieg and was followed by Shep Fields and his Rippling Rhythm. Mariko stood. Time to dance.

- Just look at them, said Mariko, on the floor. Made for each other.

- Does she?

- Of course not, was the cold answer. My girls are good girls.

- I know, I know. But, does she?

- How would I know? She's brand-new here. We haven't talked.

- You dance good, said Mr. Paul.

- You too, said Mitsuko.

- Oops, sorry. My fault.

Later, to Guy Lombardo and His Royal Canadians: You dance so well and you speak so well too. And you like our little Mitsuko-san here? Mariko asked.

- You are very beautiful, said Hiroshi, nearby, his face in Mitsuko's hair. Receiving a giggle in reply, he tightened his grip. I would like to see you alone sometime, he added. Perhaps a lunch, a dinner.

- Watanabe-san!

- Not a word, now, not a word. This is our little secret, he said, drawing away.

They then sat down and ate what Mariko said were steak tips and what were certainly fried potatoes, and the men talked business and the women talked about Mariko's problems.

Getting girls to work. So difficult these days. And the young ones with no staying power, she added, looking at the young one before her. And-they-don't-even-have-to-do-anything-they-do-not-want-to. And she stared meaningfully.

And then - oh, the years of listening to their little woes: watching the wily ones, the ones who cheated on the side; the greedy ones who ate the raisin

butter on the sly; the widows, weeping on the customers. Then the problems of the patrons: the
ones who wouldn't pay their bills; the ones who
grabbed and meant it; the show-off regulars who'd
order airfreight mangoes to impress the client and
then let them sit and rot.

All in all, a young girl was best off getting a steady
man to come and see her at her place of employment. And, here, foreigners were best really,
though they did tend to lower the tone. And there
was the disease factor too, though not, certainly
not, definitely not in this case.

Oh, the times, the times. Things were no longer
what they had been. And, as further example of loss
of standards nowadays: That monkey. Nice little
thing, gift of a guest. Fit the Arab decor too. And
the girls all fed it, bananas and things, and it used to
climb on the customers and bite. Very popular.

- Then, one day I noticed it was eating the plastic
ivy and carrying on but didn't think much of it and
next thing you know it was dead - just stretched
out there, in its little chain. You see, the girls had
gotten tired of it. They had forgotten to feed it.

- It perished in the midst of plenty, she concluded, perhaps quoting. And that is what I mean by
loss of standards nowadays. She looked sternly at
Mitsuko who gazed up guiltily as though she herself
had neglected the unfortunate simian.

These various conversations took some time. Then Hiroshi looked around, expressed surprise at the hour, checked his Seiko, and said: Well, tomorrow's a busy day for the both of us. Probably better be getting on home. And Mariko whined professionally that it was still so early and what were they thinking of, and Mr. Paul was on his feet and shaking Mitsuko's hand

Then Hiroshi was shaking Mitsuko's hand as well, holding on a bit long, and Mariko was playfully slapping at him with a large pillow on which was embroidered all of *L'Embarquement pour Cythère*, and the party broke up.

2

A few days later Mariko asked Hiroshi to take her out. He suggested several places they both knew. She, however, had decided.

- The Empire? he cried. But men can't go there!

- They can if a woman takes them, she said firmly.

So, just as the clock struck nine, the discrete brassplated door was swept open by a pin-striped young man who showed surprise, perhaps at the sight of another male, hesitated, then bowed low.

A large room - chairs and tables, plain, like a boys' dormitory. Posters of rock stars, steam engines, Marilyn Monroe, lips apart. Toilet indicated by small plaque reading Toilet.

- It lacks the woman's touch, said Mariko sitting in a camp chair behind a formica-topped table.

Hiroshi looked at the young men lounging against the walls and asked: Why did we come here?

- Because I'm in business, that's why. I wanted to find out how the other half lives. Places like this are making real money nowadays.

They were approached by a good-looking young man who touched his perm, flashed his teeth, and said: Welcome to the Empire. He then snapped his fingers and several boys brought glasses, ice, a full bottle of Johnny Walker Black, papayas, kiwis, raisin butter and Kraft on Ritz.

- It's just like your place only with men instead of women, said Hiroshi, looking at the lounging youths. Then: I wonder if they have to put out.

Mariko glanced at him, distaste apparent, and music appeared - 'How Much Is That Doggie in the Window' - and Mariko turned to the good-looking young man touching his perm.

- You are Master Minoru, I believe, she said. Then: I am Madame Mariko of the Yamato. She produced a card which the boy read, then bowed over. There was a murmur among the other lads, then a scurry in the kitchen. After some confusion (sounds of chopping, muffled shouts) there appeared: cut-up cucumbers, a watermelon, half a cold chicken on which had been dumped a jar of Miracle Whip.

- They certainly do lack the woman's touch, said Hiroshi while, sipping and picking, Mariko settled back for a talk with Master Minoru.

- You see, you got to go slow, he was saying. You got to gauge the customer. Some you got to be seduced by, like; others, you got to press like on with, and others you got to - you'll excuse the term - rape. Why? Because that's what the clientele wants, that's why.

Mariko nodded, sage, and Hiroshi, interested, asked: What if you rape one you ought to be seduced by?

Minoru tapped a smooth forehead: Inspiration. It's all up here. Either you got it or you don't. It's a business sense.

But, Hiroshi wanted to know, what about affection, and trust and, yes, love.

Mariko looked impatient; Minoru, scandalized.

- But sir, he said. This is a business. We're like a company. Look at Sony, look at Honda. Do they think about love? No, sir. Not at all. They just do their jobs. Push the product. He regarded a polished oxford, and added: You might call us real craftsmen.

Hiroshi's snort was covered by a new tune: 'The Tennessee Waltz.' Master Minoru, gallant, bowed and then swept Mariko off among the tables while Hiroshi regarded the watermelon.

Minoru danced very close and upon their return the woman said, giggling: I don't have a secret left.

- You're not supposed to. He was demonstrating the tricks of the trade.

- Really, she said, fanning herself with her hand-kerchief, then leaned forward with: Well, they have this blackboard in the kitchen and it shows who is most popular. And these widows and bar madames come in new and ask who is most popular and they are told and so they ask for him and that keeps him most popular, you see. Nice little system.

Hiroshi nodded.

- And they have all the same problems I do. The boys aren't all of them that dedicated, you see. And so, of course, they just go and put out. And that is against company rules.

Hiroshi again nodded.

- Oh, they put out all right, but only after a time, a long time, she continued. But what happens is that this company president's wife, say, comes in here just once and drags some urchin home then sets him up in an apartment and gets him a Fair

Lady. Of course, he never comes back here again. Just like my girls.

- But surely that's one of the reasons they work there, your girls, said Hiroshi reasonably: Take that Dewi Sukarno, now. She was a hostess once and the president of Indonesia made her a great lady and then went and died.

Mariko regarded him with a neutral displeasure for a moment, then said: Speaking of leaving, I hate to tell you that our Mitsuko-san of the other night just up and left herself. Really. This younger generation.

- Oh! cried Hiroshi, When, where? Then, more quietly: Wherever could she have gone, I wonder

- So do I, said Madame Mariko. Then, with a narrowing of eyes: I hear that she went to work in this lesbian bar.

- A lesbian bar? Hiroshi was surprised.

- Yes, Never can tell, can you? And she was such a good girl too. So bright. So pretty. In her way.

Minoru brought over Jun and Joji, two affable, dressed-up youths who kissed Mariko's hand and nodded at Hiroshi.

- But, said the host, I did not bring Ken over there. He indicated a handsome but solitary youth. He is just not well-bred enough for this table.

- What happened? wondered Mariko.

- Danced with the master's widow, said Jun with a giggle.

- Took home the master's cosmetic company president, said Joji with a grimace.

- Two clients, Minoru modestly explained. I had asked Ken to help out but there are limits.

Mariko smiled, nodded, shook her head, had heard it all before.

- Which lesbian bar? wondered Hiroshi, whispering.

- How would I know, said Mariko in a loud voice. Then: Oh, yes, I heard . . . called something . . . yes, called Elle.

3

Hiroshi arrived early at the Elle.

Here the woman's touch was everywhere. Little tables, tiny chairs, silvered candles, what-nots, blown-glass animals, music boxes, teddy bears, low-hanging lamps, dolls sitting, leaning, lolling, lying down - all staring.

Among these were the girls. There seemed to be several kinds. Those behind the bar wore short hair, bow ties, and looked like boys but, with their inquiring eyes, their rueful mouths, rather strange boys. And they were not pretty.

The pretty ones were of two varieties. One wore suits with cuffs, lapels, hair pulled behind ears. The other, full skirts, flowered prints, puffed sleeves, picture hats. The suited ones, effeminate gamblers, apparently brought the drinks. The pretty ones, their company. The plain ones behind the bar made the sloe gin fizzes and violet delights.

Yet peer as he might into the candled gloom, Hiroshi could not see Mitsuko, though he had asked for her. He could detect only the scornful glances of the girls and the sharp stare of the woman who had opened the portal, the Mistress herself - tall, formidable. A single man apparently did not unchallenged enter.

Music - *Swan Lake* - and Mitsuko appeared, a slice of fish cake between her teeth. Why, hello there, she said, sitting down, biting, swallowing.

- I heard you were here.

- You're my first customer. Now you have to eat and drink lots. I get ten percent.

- You'll soon be rich, he said, smiling.

- And how's the Madame? Angry? I left a little suddenly.

- Not at all. It was from her I learned you were - ah - here.

Mitsuko looked around with an understanding little smile: I'm not a dyke, you know. It's just that the money's better.

Then, unasked: Oh, it's got its drawbacks. Widows, nurses and airline hostesses - they are the worst. Hands all over you. And not like in the Yamato where the guys do it to impress each other. These girls mean business. Wow!

The Mistress appeared and whispered in her ear after which Mitsuko called over a youngster in schoolgirl uniform who received the order. Caviar, lobster mayonnaise, asparagus, mangoes and, oh, yes, Kraft on Ritz.

- Orders, the Mistress's. Sorry. She's very strict, though just a girl at heart, she says. Her name is really Hanako, but imagine calling anyone that butch that. She is terribly ashamed of it. So we have to call her just the Mistress. What? Oh no, nothing like that, no discipline if that is what you are thinking about.

Hiroshi giggled, delighted, ducking his head boyishly.

- You are really so beautiful in that dress.

- It's dotted swiss, she modestly said.

- Well, whatever, it really becomes you, he warmly replied as the schoolgirl staggered in with the food.

- So, Madame Mariko wasn't upset with me? Mitsuko asked, mouth full. Then: Do you believe in infidelity, Mr. Hiroshi?

- Well, I have a wife, you know.

- So I would imagine, at your age, she said reprovingly. But I mean infidelity against anyone you had ever really cared about.

- That might well depend upon the individuals involved, he said, smiling: Case by case, you know.

She fluffed her dotted swiss and sucked an asparagus stalk. I guess you're right. Then, kicking her heels in juvenille fashion: You're so smart. You know so much about life.

He basked. Then a few more guests arrived. She turned to look and then began telling him about the clientele here at the Elle.

The thing was to get them hooked. The Mistress always said so in her nightly pep talk. Never give out. Keep them hanging. But if they don't hang properly, give - but only a little: a look, a hand on the arm, something subtle, at the very most a tit press. That way, you see, the clientele appeared every night, or as often as they could afford to, for the Elle was very expensive.

The guests were all older: married women in groups who laughed and waved their hands about to show how at ease they were, a solitary, severely tailored woman or two who drank her whiskey straight, had a friend who worked here by whom she was studiously avoided; a few very made-up with eye shadow, in distressed jeans, noisy; others, usually in pairs, subdued in evening pants; very occasionally, once a month maybe, a lone woman, often foreign, on the prowl - always getting nowhere because lesbians did not hunt since they were by definition faithful.

- Then how do they meet in the first place? wondered Hiroshi with a waggish little grin.

This Mitsuko ignored, continuing her description: We get men too sometimes. Though they really ought to be accompanied by women. We have to be careful, you know. The kind of man who gets excited at the idea of two girls being together. Had one the other night. Full of questions. Wanted to know if we used our fingers. Or what. You're not that kind now, are you? she asked, peering closely.

- No, no, not at all, never, no, Hiroshi was saying when the Mistress appeared and whispered in Mitsuko's ear.

- She wants me to keep my voice down. And she wants me to move. We're supposed to circulate. Have to go over there.

She pointed: There, that one. She teaches high school chemistry. Her fingers are all brown. Ugh! Well, ciao.

After that Hiroshi sat for a time with the schoolgirl and discussed the weather: it was still pleasant but we must not forget that shortly the rainy season would be upon us.

4

- Yes, but how deeply is Hiroshi-san in love with Madame Mariko is what I'm asking, said Mitsuko putting down an unsipped Shirley Temple.

- I do not know. They have been together. Years. She is strong. He is rich.

Having said this, Mr. Paul looked around at the well-bred boys with their their buttoned collars and argyle socks, their folded hands and downcast eyes, and asked: Why are we here?

- Oh, said Mitsuko, girlishly kicking her feet against the fake oak bar and gazing around at the tartan and the hunting prints: I work in this dyke bar so I couldn't ask you there. Foreigners are all right, of course, but they've got to be women too, you see. Anyway, I'm always with these lesbians so I wanted to find out how the other half lives in case I ever go into business for myself.

- You want Hiroshi to buy you a bar, stated Paul.

- That's what I like about you foreigners. Right to the point. Well, yes, but we must not leave out romance.

One of the boys raised his eyes, reached in front of Paul for the cashews and then excused himself. In English.

- That's what they like here at the Regency, I am told, said Mitsuko conversationally. Foreign faggots. That is why they wear Brooks Brothers and speak English.

- This is a strange place to take a date, observed Paul, turning away from the young man who was staring at him, his mouth full, his heart apparently fuller.

- But they don't allow girls here without men, explained Mitsuko and the boy tossed his head, swallowed his nuts, and turned away.

- He heard you speak Japanese, she said. You are not authentic, he thinks. He will wait until a real one comes in.

- He'll wait. Not many here.

- It's probably AIDS, she explained. That must really hurt the business. You know, like botulism in that wedding banquet hall last year. They went bankrupt finally.

Mitsuko was certain that the homo business was way off. Problem was one of supply and demand. All these boys were only interested in foreigners, middle-aged persons from Cailfornia, last of the type, who wandered in wearing bell-bottoms, sideburns, with medallions clinking, and wearing too a single expression: big spender in the whorehouse.

They would stare at the prim counter, then move in. A word of English, maybe a sentence. Then, from the Japanese side, a start of surprise, a careful reply to show how polite and well-bred one was. And so on, further proceedings being conducted with the gravity of a major merger.

- Yes, said Paul. Japanese want out, foreigner wants in.

- That's right, said Mitsuko. But right now what with AIDS and the high prices homos just aren't turning up anymore. At least not in the numbers necessary.

- But the strange thing, continued Mitsuko, reverting, is that neither wants any money. That's the really funny thing about homos. At the Elle a girl who gets taken out comes back rich. Except that she has to cough up to the Mistress, of course. But a bar like this one only makes money on turnover. And there is not that much turnover now. See? You are the only foreigner here. That is why you are so popular.

Then, perhaps, logically: By the way, did you know that I was intended for you that night?

- Yes. I thought so. Probably.

- But it was not fated to be, she said, perhaps quoting.

- No. You were interested in Hiroshi-san.

- Did it show? She giggled. Then: How come you speak better Japanese now than then ?
- I am going to study.
- I am studying, she corrected.
- Really? What? he wanted to know and after she had said, no, no, not me, you, they talked on, she correcting his Japanese from time to time.
- What I don't understand is the finances of a place like this, she said. It's got to be turnover. So many boys, so few foreigners. And the kids just got to keep on coming until they hit. Like pachinko.

She turned to ask a bow-tied youth in saddle oxfords while Paul avoided the advances of a sloe-eyed youth in a seersucker suit.

- Yes, she said, turning back: And before AIDS it was just the opposite. All foreigners and no boys. A run on the market. Will you kindly mind your own business?

This to the seersucker youth who was leaning heavily against Paul. Then: Of course, he's been with her for simply ages. You'd think he'd get tired. She's not as young as she once was, you know.
- Hiroshi? He's afraid.
- Of her? Well, I wouldn't be surprised. Mitsuko giggled and began stroking Paul's hand right there in public and scandalizing all the boys. These looked at the bartender in mute outrage.
- Oh, is that the bill? They want us to go? She

giggled and slid off her stool. But I am not going to give up on this. I have reason to believe he rather likes me. No, no, silly. You never leave a tip. Never. And certainly not after you've been kicked out.

Then they both laughed until they had opened the fake oak door and stood, with no umbrellas, looking at the full, heavy, falling curtain. The rainy season had arrived.

5

- Oh, and it gets in the drapes and the backs fall off books and the piano came unglued at the Rat Mort and one of the strings lashed out and caught Momoko right here.

Mariko pointed where, going on as she did every year about the rainy season, while Hiroshi sat in one of the faux-Empire chairs and the sound of water reached even deep into the interior of the Yamato.

- There! Look! She indicated a spot on the damask-covered walls. It sweats, you see. It's just concrete underneath and so the water comes right through.

Isn't that revolting? Oh, I have to do something.

Hiroshi nodded, as though he knew what it was she had to do, as though he had heard this all before. When she said: I have simply got to remodel, he nodded his head a final time, grimly.

- Oh, look at that face. It won't cost all that much.

- Still Japanese?

- I'm thinking of it.

- Then it will cost that much. You know what wood costs these days.

- Oh, I don't mean real wood, silly. They've got this photographed stuff now. Looks really real if you don't touch it. And plastic shoji so we wouldn't have to change the paper all the time. And me in a kimono!

He looked at her as though he could not imagine this. Pouting, she sat on his lap and the Empire chair groaned. Then she pinched him affectionately and said: Did you know that your great friend Mr. Paul had the kindness to take out our little Mitsuko?

Hiroshi started, Mariko gripped, the chair creaked.

- Where? he asked.

- A rather strange place, he said.

- He said? You seeing him too?

She threw back her head and gave her famous throaty laugh. Silly. He comes here sometimes.

Brings business guests.

- Brings his guests here? But this is my place. I brought him here!

- This is my place, she reminded him, with dignity, standing up.

- But we're in the same business. He'll be bringing my clients here next thing I hear.

Midori struck her head from the kitchen and called.

When Mariko returned she was shaking her head. That girl. You'd think she'd get herself a new dress instead of fussing with that zipper all the time.

- Where did he take her?

- Well, she took him it would appear. And to some faggot place. Like your friend Saburo's, she added.

- Saburo is no faggot. He and I were in the same graduating class at university. Besides, he just owns the place. Those places make money because so many perverts don't want to go home. Anyway, you know Saburo as well as I do.

- Ha-ha. A bit better, perhaps, seeing as how he is no faggot, as you say. No, no, no, you are not to be jealous. First jealous of Paul and now of Saburo. No, no, no, she said, laughing lightly and again falling into his lap.

After they had picked themselves up off the parquet and Mariko had angrily shooed away Midori and Emiko who had heard the crash and rushed in, Hiroshi looked at the pieces and said: That chair was not very well made.

- It was an antique, a real antique, wailed Mariko. Now we've simply got to remodel.

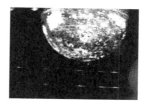

Umbrellas left, then up the spiral staircase, drenched oxfords, dripping wedgies, soaked summer pants and damp thighs dappled with reflections from all the mirrors, all the spangles, all the shaking sequins. And at the top, a burst of laser, a barrage of rock as the giant neon Titania bent down and with her magic wand and a blinding blast of strobe, touched the portal.

- But I wanted to talk, yelled Hiroshi.

- What? shouted Mitsuko, deafened as she stared.

Wall to wall pomaded temples, hair pulled back, pony tails; punk spikes; a sack suit with epaulettes; a pair of breasts bouncing irrespective; a tank top with "Kiss It" in day-glo; dancing dog tags and a surplus safari hat, all dappled by the swinging lights and the beat, the beat, covering everything.

The pair was led through the writhing dancers, among the steel beams, ducking under all the hi-tech look, to a small table just vacated by three apparent twelve-year-olds in pigtails and someone even younger in fringes.

- I thought we could have a nice quiet talk, shouted Hiroshi.

- You did? asked Mitsuko. But isn't the music good though?

- I can't hear you for the awful noise!

Sudden silence. The young people stood limp, crowded, sweating, waiting.

- It looks like a disaster, a grade-school mass drowning, he said.

- It's the Titania, the most popular discotheque in all of Akasaka, said Mitsuko virtuously.

He nodded. I've heard of it. This is where Kawabata used to come before he killed himself.

- I knew a woman saw him here, said Mitsuko. Said he always sat in the corner, always in full kimono. And staring - big white eyes. Used to watch the young girls so hard he looked blind.

- And he took them out afterwards, ventured Hiroshi.

- Yes, but not like the newspapers said. He only

took them for sundaes at the Hotel Okura. That's what this woman told me. Then: I read *Snow Country* once. Its about this geisha -

Mitsuko seemed about to recount the plot, so Hiroshi said: I am glad you could come out with me. Was the Mistress difficult?

- Oh, no. I just told her my mother was ill.
- That's good, said Hiroshi, with a little smile
- Actually she's dead.

He stopped smiling: Was she that ill?

- No, no, that was years ago, when I was little. I just told Madame Mariko I had had one, you see. It's more respectable.

- So you live all by your little self, said Hiroshi. Then as though this naturally followed: Actually, I've been wanting to talk with you.

- Me too. You see, I didn't know you were married.

- Married? he asked surprised. But of course. What's that got to do with anything? Who told you that?

- Mr. Paul.
- You see him very much?
- Oh, a little, from time to time, she said carefully.
- Well, I'd be careful. He took you to a gay bar.
- No, I took him.

Whatever Hiroshi had been going to add was blasted away by another explosion. At once every-one was gyrating. So, after several attempts at conversation, he took her to the floor. Here his fox trot occasioned collisions and so she danced by herself, fingers snapping, head thrown about, while he shuffled.

Back at the table he looked around: How do you get a drink here:

- One is included with each admission, said Mitsuko, quoting.

- But who is going to bring it? he wondered. In the distance were several youths holding trays and chatting.

- I am sure your wife is a lovely person, said Mitsuko suddenly.

- Yes, I suppose so. Me, I do pretty much what I want.

- And Miss Mariko is a lovely person, she added. You are fortunate. Two such lovely ladies in your life.

- I want a drink, said Hiroshi, looking around. And it's too hot in here.

- All the bodies.

At once they were galvanized by yet another blast, guitars screaming, cymbals crashing, while Hiroshi waved unsuccessfully at passing waiters. Over the racket he shouted: No wonder Kawabata committed suicide.

- No, no, screamed Mitsuko in answer: It was love, love he wanted. It's love everyone wants. Me too, I only want someone to love me.

The music suddenly stopped and Mitsuko's 'love me' sailed out into the silence. Two girls in T-shirts turned to look and a small boy in a beanie, surprised, stuck out his tongue, while a waiter, concerned, hurried over, brought two cherry Cokes as though they were antidote itself and said: Better drink up.

- Oh, it's all over, cried Mitsuko.

So it was. The DJs were packing up, and wiping off sweat, buttoning up flies, the ponytails, the punk spikes, the jeans and patches were all disappearing down the spiral staircase as though down a drain.

- You mean someplace actually closes at night in Tokyo? asked Hiroshi, surprised, belching on the hasty Coke.

- It's the new law, she said, the growing young having to study and all, future mothers and fathers of Japan. Then she shook her head: Feels like I got water in my ears. Is it true that all the young are deaf now? That the music eats away the eardrums?

- Sounds like it, said Hiroshi, guiding her down the spiral staircase, their footsteps echoing in the silence. Overhead the giant Titania, now dead, bent, spent wand in hand.

- You're not to be jealous of Mr. Paul, said Mitsuko suddenly. I am independent. I do as I want. My way.

- You'll go out with me again?
- If your, ah, lady friend permits.
- I am independent. I do as I want. My way.
She laughed.
- All the way, he added, heavily.
And they stepped out into the rain.

7

- Oh, the rain. My hair. Can't do anything with it.
She shook her mane, gave her famous throaty laugh, and both Hiroshi and Paul looked at her and smiled. Then: Oh, I just love this place. So refined.
The Starlight Lounge of the Hotel Continental-Marunouchi was low and long and Tokyo twinkled below the wide windows. Waiters glided through the gloom and in one subdued corner Satch (Happy) Suzuki and his Streamliners sounded. At present it was 'Don't Get Around Much Anymore.'
- And it just never changes. So reassuring, continued Mariko with a firm nod of approval, concluding with: And so foreign you think you're in a real foreign country. See, look at all the foreigners here.

- One is at your table, said Paul, candid.

Mariko smiled fondly and pressed his hand then, suddenly arch, looked at Hiroshi: No, no, no, you are not to be jealous. Here Mr. Paul is being so Japanese. Returning our hospitality like this, you see. He is such a good friend. Like family. And so understanding. Almost a real Japanese himself, though perhaps one from a better former time what with his liking for all our old-fashioned things. Oh, no, Hiroshi-san, if you want to be jealous you will just have to be jealous about someone else.

As though taking advice, Hiroshi turned to Paul and said: I understand you have been seeing Mitsuko-san.

- Once, said Paul. She took me out. She had something she wanted to talk about.

He stared in a manner perhaps meaningful as he said this.

- Oh, no, cried Mariko, having perhaps interpreted the stare, and the headwaiter hurried over, perhaps thinking the guest had found something in her food.

- Miss Mitsuko, stated Mariko, is to do precisely as she wants. Even though it may mean breaking her various promises with me. She is free certainly to see anyone she wants.

- Anyone? asked Hiroshi.

- Anyone. Besides, she's a lesbian, said Mariko, as

though to the hovering headwaiter, who hastily retired.

- She is working there, said Mr. Paul.

- Where there's smoke there's fire, was the dark rejoinder.

After that they ate their corn soup, their chicken à la king, their lettuce with mayonnaise and their apple pie.

- Just like being in America, Mariko marveled.

During coffee (American, nice and weak, how delicious) she remembered: What did you mean by that anyone?

- Anyone?

- Anyone. You said anyone. Who is that?

- Me? asked Hiroshi.

Yes, you. You said that Mitsuko-san could see just anyone.

- No, no. it was you who said that.

- Yes, I said that. But you said it after me. What did you mean by that?

- More pie? American! stated Mr. Paul.

Not to be dissuaded, seemingly suspicious, Mariko waved a dismissive hand at their friend the foreigner and stared at the Japanese.

- He is up to something again, she said. About once every two years. I can always tell.

Then, seeing that their foreign host was about to speak, perhaps to protest: No, no. You are close enough to know our secrets. You are almost one of our group, and, sad as it is to admit, we Japanese have our shame as well. And a part of it is our men. They all behave like this. And her a lesbian, she concluded.

More pie was again proffered, and again refused, but a bit of the American brew was allowed and Satch (Happy) Suzuki and his Streamliners played 'Chattanooga Choo-Choo.'

Returning from the dance-floor Mariko smiled, pecked Paul a kiss, and said to Hiroshi: Well, your foreign friend can't talk all that good but he dances much, much better than you do.

Then they laughed and after a time Mariko said she had had a perfectly lovely time and thank you so very much.

Satch (Happy) Suzuki and his Streamliners were playing 'Don't Get Around Much Anymore,' and Mitsuko looked wonderingly about. Oh, she said, it is just like being in a foreign land.

Tokyo twinkled below them and there was, in addition, a large moon, a short respite in the rainy season having occurred. The two were eating chicken à la king.

- And foreign food, too, she added.

- And all you need now is a foreign gentleman, said Hiroshi, surly. Someone like Mr. Paul, right?

- Oh, no, she cried, and the headwaiter started in her direction then, apparently considering, stopped. You are not to behave this way, spoiling my perfectly lovely evening (here she stabbed at her iceberg lettuce) and such a nice night, too, she added, glancing at the moon.

- Yes, it is a nice little place, isn't it? Use it all the time. Might call it my place. I even bring my clients here now. Brought Yamada-san in the other day. He liked it. Said it was just like a foreign country.

Mitsuko looked up, eyes wide, teeth apparent and said that some time, just once, she would like to see a real foreign country, and then, with a little smile, bent seriously, schoolgirl-like, over her apple pie.

Hiroshi with a knowing air said that it was not impossible that she might someday view a real foreign land for all he knew. At which she looked up, eyes shining.

- Yes, foreign lands, continued Hiroshi. They are all right. But foreigners themselves. Well, I just don't know. I have so often wondered if they can truly understand us. They are, you see, after all, foreign.

She nodded her head, waiting, empty, dumb.

- The way I see it, he said, foreigners are perfectly all right. I know lots. He waved his hand, indicating the Starlight Lounge. Many of my friends are foreigners. And yet, and yet. When it comes to inner feelings, well, then, I just wonder, you see. After all, we Japanese understand each other. We think with our stomachs, I believe the saying goes. Our inner feelings are apparent, or should be. Here he smiled as though to indicate the apparent quality of his for her.

- And so - he concluded - I just wonder, sort of, when I see a good, well brought-up girl like yourself taking up with one of them. And at a faggot bar, too. And there is the health angle to take into consideration.

- Mr. Paul's not a faggot, I don't think, she said, sitting up.

- Where there's smoke there's fire, you might say.

- And as for the health angle I read in *Girls' Own* that since we Japanese all drink miso soup we're OK.

- Not, said Hiroshi, following a logic of his own, that I think you are a lesbian just because you work in a lesbian bar. Not at all. Not - at - all.

- I am not a lesbian, said Mitsuko with simple dignity.

- There, you see, said Hiroshi, smiling broadly. More pie?

- No, no. I would die. It was just too delicious. And this place, this Starlight Lounge is it?, how did you ever find it?

Hiroshi waved his hands about expansively. Oh, I just somehow hear about little out-of-the-way places like this. Again he waved expansively and the headwaiter rushed over, already bent double, to hear the complaint.

- No, no, no, cried Hiroshi, once he had understood and Mitsuko in her merriment swallowed wrong a bit of pie and had to have her back pounded by both before she coughed it up.

- Oh, I'm so embarrassed, she said once the waiter was gone.

- Have some water. Poor thing. You are pale. Look, I am going to take you home.

- Oh, no, I'm all right.

- You ought to be in bed.

- Oh, no.

- Can't have you getting sick. I want to see you all tucked in.

So they left the Starlight Lounge and on the way out Hiroshi actually tipped Satch (Happy) Suzuki and his Streamliners.

9

- Why did you take me here, shouted Hiroshi. I wanted to talk with you.

The Honolulu Cabaret, the Ueno branch - women squealing, men shouting, speakers blaring old Misora Hibari, one small person popping up, saying: Hi, my name is Momoko and I want to shake hands.

- Just thought I'd check how it was going, said Saburo Tanaka. These places make money, you know.

Momoko pushed forward. No, no, no, said Hiroshi.

- I can shake hands with my pussy, said Momoko proudly: Shake!

- Later, girls, later, said Saburo with his boyish grin. Friend and I just want to talk.

- Talk? shouted the girls above the din and then looked at each other with round, mystified eyes.

Far in the back, away from the crowd, away from Momoko, Hiroshi turned in a serious manner to his friend.

- I need your help, he began, seeing as how we

are such old classmates, same old alma mater all
those years.

Then he stopped, considered, began again: Well,
you know Mariko. Lovely person. Knew too you
always had a yen for her, as it were. Probably kept
away because you knew about our little arrange-
ment, hers and mine. But, you know, seeing as how
you're such an old friend and . . .

Here Saburo interrupted: Getting a bit much, eh?

Hiroshi nodded, miserable, then, seriously: But
don't get me wrong. A good girl, a grand person,
as you well know.

But here they were discovered by Momoko and
her hordes. The sweaty girls swarmed, ordered
beer, dried squid, fish cake and Kraft on Ritz, then
set about entertaining the customers. Momoko
was particularly desirous to demonstrate her talent. After they had been again driven off and the
beer mopped up, Saburo with a look around began
talking about the economics of the place.

- The Honolulu Cabaret is a chain, you know, he
began, and Hiroshi shook his head, perhaps thinking
of Momoko multifold. They get the money on
extras, you see. After you've drunk your beer, the
one drink you get on your ticket, the girls all order
more, and they've got this way of computing the
bills here that really adds up. Not a bad little system.

- Girls get anything? Hiroshi wondered.

- Just the ordinary ten percent, but they'll do almost anything to get it.

- So I saw, said Hiroshi, feeling the damp trousers Momoko had spilt beer on trying to get into.

- Girls are better off elsewhere, of course, continued Saburo. Look at the other places, he said knowledgeably, and then went on to discuss them.

These low-class clubs with girls in everything but the soup and all of them getting a pittance. And, then the negligée salons where they sat in their single garment in the gloom, and allowed liberties taken for very little. Next the handkerchief salons where, in similar gloom, it was the girls who took the liberties, all for peanuts, nimbly catching the results in a fresh white hankie which was then neatly folded and stuck into the breast pocket upon departure, a souvenir of the visit.

Then the simple whores, pimp-ridden, in pub or alley whose conversation was eternally the fee or the ill-fitting pumps. And the shops where one took Polaroids of the quivering organ. And others where impressions were made on white washi paper with black sumi ink, works which the girls would sometimes sign, but for which they would receive little indeed.

And then the strip-shows where the girls called out and members of the audience (company lapel pins firmly reversed) trod the boards. The act of love, accompanied by a military march and cries of encouragement or derision from the others watching this accomplished, the pearly condom waved in proof, satisfied customer stuffed back into his underwear, next girl waiting in the wings. And all for nothing - oh, some, but the management took the most.

- So, I just got out, concluded Saburo. You can't keep decent girls that way. That's when I got into boys, you see. No problem. All you do is provide this venue for the customers to act up in. No one expects any money and so you get all the profit - and a quick turnover too. Homosexuality, no mistake, is Japan's greatest growth industry. My Lovely Boy pays off. Course I have to keep a couple of guys around who go out for money. That's for the really ugly customers or if they're spastic or something.

His listener nodded, appreciating business acumen when he saw it. There is, however, the disease factor, he remarked.

- Just keep the foreigners out and the problem is solved.

- But perhaps, among the native guests -

- Nope, something about all that miso soup.

- Ah, yes, said Hiroshi, I think I heard about that.

Then, with a smile he began talking from his own years of experience: The Yamato's really quite different, he began.

It was the fault of society, really, the fact that girls never stayed. They had been encouraged to expect marriage, you see, or at least something more permanent than sitting in a club every night.

Oh, their hopes. These he well knew. If only they could be taken, out, off, away. And this was where they made their money too, being taken out. The bar had to be paid, the madame was paid, and the girls were paid. And then something more might come of all this money spent - marriage, kids, or at least an apartment.

And wasn't that why these poor girls encouraged intimacies? The hug, the peck, the sniff, the scratch. Yes, encouraged. Poor creatures. They had but one ambition, to be someone's mistress, at least, and quit this awful job.

These girls, oh, the lives they led. Night butterflies, they were called - a pretty phrase, but pretty its reality was not. And then the awful rivalry, the competition was worse than that of any automobile company, even.

Yes. Hiroshi knew all about this, knew too all the trials of poor Mariko. Yes, indeed. Poor thing.

- So you want me to keep the little woman out of the way, then, said Saburo, reverting.

- Not at all. I only thought that since we're such old friends -

- Got it. Sure. Then: You got someone else on

the side? Hiroshi drew himself up as though in denial, then collapsed: Yes.

- Anyone I know? What's her name?

- Certainly not, said Hiroshi, as though virtuously. Then, with a defeated smile: I'm counting on you. Then: Mitsuko.

- Mitsuko, eh?

And at the door the girls screamed and Momoko rode the unwilling Hiroshi's damp leg halfway into the wet and darkened street.

10

- Hiroshi, said Mitsuko, eyes half-closed, as though viewing a distant prospect.

- I gave up 'A Mother's Heart,' the eighty-second episode, said her friend Sumire, blinking her little eyes.

- It's only the tube. You watch too much of that. Not good for you.

- It won the Education Ministry Prize last year, 'A Mother's Heart' did, said Sumire as though defending. And I never missed a single one until tonight except when my mother came up from the country to see me. She can't stand it. It's about this mother, you see, and her problems -

- Don't tell me the plot.

- Oh, I couldn't. It's so complicated. Anyway, I always cry a lot. But I don't mind missing it, you understand. One can cry any time. And I did want to hear about this Hiroshi person. Such a nice name, she added, sipping her strawberry shake, again blinking.

They were in My Kitty, a place called a bar for the very young, which served things such as crêpes with ice cream cheese soup, and kitten burgers. Around the two girls sat the very young, smacking and slurping.

Sumire concluded with: And he likes you too?

- I have reason to so believe, said Mitsuko with a mysterious smile.

- Wow, said Sumire.

- He's taken me out. To the Starlight Lounge.

- The what?

- You wouldn't know it. It's one of the better places.

Sumire shook her head in simple wonder: I wouldn't know it, she repeated seriously.

- Satch (Happy) Suzuki and his Streamliners entertain there nightly, Mitsuko added.

- Who?

- There, you see?

After a time Sumire reached the bottom of her strawberry shake, slurped and said: But, you've not gone the whole way yet.

- Oh, no. Not yet.

- Will you?

- Really, what a question. Only-if-I-have-to.

- What if you really have to then?

- Then, you'll just have to, said the waiter, a long, acned youth, as he removed shake glass and plate.

- Really, said Mitsuko in disapproval: This place is losing its tone.

Both girls peered about. American McDonald-style interior, all reds and yellows, stuffed animals everywhere, and lots of paper napkins with My Kitty on them for the sloppy young. Outside the windows all Harajuku passed. The door opened with a merry chime and two very young boys in studs, spikes and leather walked in.

- See? said Mitsuko. There goes the tone.

- But they are children, said Sumire.

- You just wait, said Mitsuko darkly. Anyway, there is a problem.

- Not really, if you just tell the management.

- No, no. I meant with Hiroshi-san. You'll understand if I don't divulge his last name. Anyway, there is this other woman.

- Yes, where you work. The Mistress.

- Yes, she is a problem. She likes me too, I think.

But I meant another woman.

- Another woman, said Sumire, shaking her head, then as though comprehending: The other woman!

- Yes, much older; in fact, old.

- Older than him even?

- No, silly, than me.

Sumire, who was younger than Mitsuko, shook her head in simple wonder at the ways of adult life.

- Look, said the elder sharply: You are only one year younger than I am. Is My Kitty going to your head?

- I am seventeen, said Sumire virtuously. Then: Go on.

- Well. I have this feeling he is going to take me out.

- I thought he had

- No, going to take me someplace and make his attempt.

- Well, will you?

- Only if I have to.

- Then, you'll just have to, said the acned waiter. You girls want to order anything more?

- This place is really on its way down, said Mitsuko loudly as she stood up and swept through the door, Sumire, having paid, pattering after.

Then she cocked her little head, looked up at the leaden sky. At least the rain has stopped for a time, she said.

11

- Wa! cried Hiroshi boyishly as they dashed into the foyer of the Colonial Inn, then stood, dripping, looking out at the solid falling curtain.

- Some rain! he said, enthusiastically.

- It's the rainy season, said Mitsuko, as though explaining.

- Well, here we are. Bet you're hungry, a growing girl like you. Hear the food's pretty good here.

This was not true, as Hiroshi well knew, having often patronized the place. The food was, in fact, widely known to be quite bad, expensive though it was, but the dining rooms were private and there was in each an ample foldout bed/sofa.

Mitsuko gazed about her after they had been discreetly ushered in. It is like being in someone's home, she said, looking at the full-color photo of Mount Fuji, at the pretty Sagi Musume doll in its glass case, at the stuffed fish, at the big color television, at the mikes and speakers for sing-along karaoke, at the picture of some foreigner (famous perhaps) frowning in the corner.

- Not bad, not bad at all, said Hiroshi chewing manfully. French cook, I hear, he said, hiding the gristle in his napkin.

- Oh, really? said Mitsuko who, having adopted a faraway and mysterious air, kept looking into the distance, playing with her hair with one hand while she managed the fork, little finger straight out, with the other.

- You look like a real TV personality, said Hiroshi.

- Oh, Watanabe-san, she said, smiling, showing her white, square, even teeth. Then. You have been here before?

- Yes, occasionally' he said carefully. Come here for the cuisine.

She nodded and gave up on the steak. Probably with Madame Mariko, I would guess, she softly guessed.

He paused, as though remembering: Yes, I guess so, a couple of times at any rate, though some time ago now.

This was another lie. He came often. Often. Mariko insisting. Either this or the Imperial. Nothing less. Since the Imperial cost a bit more and included no food and you had to spend the night or look funny checking out, Hiroshi tended to favor the Colonial.

Also, it was culturally interesting. Some of the rooms, he had discovered, had round beds, with round sheets even, which rotated at the touch of a finger. Others had a slide into the bath down which Mariko had more than once squealed. And, in addition, each and every room had a picture of a different American president.

The room Hiroshi had taken for himself and Mitsuko was initially, reassuringly, like a rather crowded dining room until, with a touch of a button, the foldout sofa, big as a bed, would spring out. Then one had to take care of one's ankles.

The waiter brought in the ice-cold hot American apple pie and the almost equally cold hot coffee. He then hovered staring until Hiroshi sent him scurrying with a jerk of the chin.

Then, turning to Mitsuko with a smile: Yes, a little like Keiko Matsushita, he said, naming a well-known actress

- Oh, she is so old, said the girl, elaborately distasteful.

- Well, Keiko Matsushita when she was a child, he said.

She giggled. So did he, then moved around to her side of the table.

 So pleasant, he said. You know, I get lonely from time to time.

- Yes, she said simply: You being a company president and all. But, you have Madame Mariko.

- Oh, no. She has her own life. Her own interests. I do not deny that we are close. Yes, very close. But, after all, it is not as though we were married.

- Oh, no, said Mitsuko simply: Particularly seeing as how you are already married.

- Yes, there is that too. But a man gets lonely. He needs an understanding woman. And he looked deep into her eyes. Hiroshi had with some success employed this ploy before.

- I don't know if I am old enough to be called a woman, said Mitsuko with a mysterious smile.

- All right then. A girl. A simple girl. How is that? A simple understanding young lady.

She giggled. So did he, then put his arm around the back of her chair. He was in no hurry, having paid for the room until midnight. And she was in no hurry either, having decided, perhaps, merely to appear reluctant. Consequently it was not until some time later that, sweaty the both of them, hands sticky, they were ready for their first kiss.

He leaned over carefully, arm about her neck, one foot in the air, finger poised to press the button at the very moment their lips touched. The moment came. He kissed her, pushed the button, the sofa shot out, the door opened, and there stood Mariko trembling with what appeared rage.

- Ow, ow, ow, yelled Hiroshi hopping about, the sofa having caught his ankle. Mitsuko stood up, instantly guilty. Mariko advanced.

- So I see how my trust is valued, she cried, as though this was a line of dialogue, and the room itself a stage. This is what your affection means.

The lines sounded practiced and perhaps they were. Hiroshi's, however, were not. Ow, ow, ow, he said, then: What? Who? How?

- The waiter, of course. That is what friends are for.

- Wait till I get my hands on -

- Ah-hah. Then you admit your guilt. You admit that this is not an innocent tête-à-tête.

She spoke with some force. The other waiters gathered at the open door. Coolidge trembled.

- And what greets my eyes? The guilty sofa unfolded. And you - ungrateful girl who quit my Yamato. But now I understand. From the very first, you two, etc.

Mariko continued, clawing the air, while Hiroshi, backed into the guilty sofa, sat down, and Mitsuko with a little cry escaped out into the rain.

12

- And I could have caught my death, said Mitsuko. Drink up. The Mistress is watching.

- I nearly caught mine, said Hiroshi, miserable. Who would have thought that that man remembered.

- What man?

- That man who served us our supper, that's who. The spy.

- Did you tip him?

- Of course not.

- She probably did. This is a racket they've got, I hear.

- You know a lot about it, he said as though bitterly.

- Only what I read in the weeklies, she said virtuously.

- Well, why did you call me to come over here? I don't feel comfortable here.

And indeed the gamblers were staring and the pretty ones peering and the plain ones glaring.

- But I wanted to know what we should do.

- What do you mean? said Hiroshi, frowning.

- Our getting caught like that.

- Caught? We weren't doing anything. Just a friendly dinner.

- But she saw.

- She saw what? he shouted.

The Mistress appeared, whispered in Mitsuko's ear.

- She wants you to keep your voice down. She

says she has a refined clientele. Also, she wants you to order.

- Order? He looked at the loaded table before him: Chivas Regal, fresh orange juice, kiwis, mangoes, and a chocolate cake.

- What shall we do? wondered Mitsuko, reverting.

- Lay low for a little while, said Hiroshi.

- Lay low from what? she wanted to know. I'm a good girl.

- I know, I know.

Mitsuko looked doubtful. I don't know just what to do. And then there is the Mistress.

- What about her? asked Hiroshi, glancing at that severely tailored and frowning woman who was now steadily regarding them.

- Well, I'm afraid she likes me.

Hiroshi seemed to be thinking of this, perhaps even relishing it. But he merely said: Well, just refuse.

- But this is my job, you see. Unlike yourself I am just a poor working person. You must understand that. I am not independent. I do not have my own place, Hiroshi-san.

And outside the rain poured.

13

It was still raining several days later, had turned humid as well, when Hiroshi was again summoned to the Yamato. He sat on a pouffe looking miserable while Midori talked about how hot it was, from time to time touching a moist upper lip with a designer handkerchief.

- Ah, there you are, said Mariko, suddenly, dramatically appearing from the kitchen. Oh, about that zipper, she began seeing Midori, then: No, later, later. Leave us alone,

Alone with Hiroshi, she said: I have been seriously thinking about the remodeling.

He nodded, miserable: I thought you probably had.

- Yes. All shoji here, and in this room full tatami, fusuma over there. Maybe a suit of samurai armor in the corner. Think of it, imagine the novelty. Opening and closing all the shoji, sliding on tatami with your shoes on, actually squatting in the toilet. Then, grandly: Yes, roots. That is what the new Yamato will be about.

She suddenly smiled and he, as though emboldened, smiled back. At once she frowned: That is why I called you over. To talk about the remodeling, she said severely.

- I see. He sat small on his pouffe.

- Just a business talk, she said. You see I am not going to mention what I saw. Not a word. I am going to say nothing about my seeing you and that person in that bed, lips glued.

- We weren't in bed.

- But you would have been.

- And it was a sofa.

- And her a lesbian, said Mariko as though scandalized.

- If she was a lesbian, said Hiroshi, suddenly acute, then nothing at all was happening.

- Oh, you can't tell about them. Lesbians are deep, was the frowning reply. Besides I saw what I saw. Eyes tell no lies, she added, perhaps quoting.

A few customers appeared and Mariko, suddenly all smiles, went to welcome them and to distribute a few of the girls. When she returned, she said: Oh, such a nice thing has happened. Just when I was feeling seriously neglected, your old classmate Saburo quite suddenly, out of nowhere, asked me out.

Hiroshi showed careful surprise. She nodded, smiling. He then showed graduated pleasure but remembered to say: Well, as long as it's not too often.

- Wait! Mariko went to Midori's rescue. The guest of a client had not realized that her hand on his thigh was there only for form's sake. The mauled Midori, zipper gaping, was replaced by the experienced and gold-toothed Emiko who would be perfectly safe with any guest.

Returned, Mariko resumed. What do you mean, as long as it's not so often? You are a fine one to talk, I must say.

Then, after a silence: Saburo is not really homo is he?

- No more than Miss Mitsuko is lesbian, was the reply.

Upon hearing this, Mariko frowned, perhaps because it was to her advantage to believe the girl homosexual and the man not.

- Silly, she finally stated.

14

- And there he was in bed with that notorious lesbian, said Mariko dramatically, eyes flashing. And there I was, a witness to their shame.

- How deep was their shame? asked Saburo.

- I beg your pardon?

- How far had he gotten? Him and this lesbian.

- In bed, my dear, in bed. Must I give the details?

- Yes, do. I would like to hear them, he said with his habitual smile, boyish, head cocked.

- Oh, you, she said and slapped at him. Then: But seriously now, it was something of a shock. You see, Watanabe-san and myself are very old friends.

- Yes. Us too, him and me, classmates, matter of fact. He's told me already what happened.

At once Mariko smoothly continued with: And so, it wasn't as though they were actually in bed together, as you'll understand, but that it was very incriminating. Very. The sofa was there. He had his lips glued to hers.

- Where? asked Saburo perhaps facetiously.

- Where?

- Well, you said she was lesbian.

- Oh! Really! You are awful. Oh. Ha-ha-ha. Mariko clawed the air and in her merriment upset her Napoleon.

Instantly a young man in full formal kimono knelt, mopped. They were having a little drink in the Higashi no Ki, an elegant establishment where all of the young men knelt all of the time whether taking orders, delivering them, or cleaning up after the clientele.

Recovered, she looked about appreciatively. There were old traditional farming tools acting as receptacles for bunches of bouquets, rustic buckets holding the champagne, real rope noren, greasy with the decades, that had to be parted before one could use either the otoko or the onna.

- They've gone traditional very nicely here, said Mariko. I really might take a few hints from how they've gone about it. What's that? She pointed: That naked woman.

- That is a real Foujita.

- There, you see? Old Japan. They've done it so well, and an old beggar's bowl to hold the soap in the ladies. Quite nicely thought out.

- You come here often? she next asked Saburo.

- Yes, I use it to bring the clients to. It impresses them. Particularly if it's a good night. You know, movie stars, TV personalities, minor royalty.

- Royalty?

- Yes, Princess Suga used to be seen here. Of course, he added, the Imperial Household put a stop to it eventually but she had fun while it lasted.

Mariko was impressed. Her eyes had a contemplative cast as though she was thinking of royalty at the refurbished Yamato.

Looking around she wondered: A good night?

- Still a bit early, said Saburo. The famous folk always come late.

- And all this rain too. Would you believe it? Nearly July and this continual downpour. Terrible at my place. Basement, you know. Mildew everywhere, and a leak in the *hommes*. Seriously, what should I do?

- About Hiroshi? asked Saburo, quick, as usual. Well, he's reached a certain age, you know. You might give him a little breathing space, as it were. And, if he wants to play around on the side, why then you could do the same thing.

- Saburo-san, what are you suggesting?

He gave her his boyish grin.

- You look good enough to eat, he said softly.

- Oh, dear! And she leaned back, nearly upsetting the kneeling youth who had come to fill her snifter. Sorry. But they do go down so suddenly, she said to Saburo.

- Master's idea. He thought people would like to be bowed to. Tried full obeisances for a while, you know, those formal three-fingered bows—but the boys complained. Always getting their hands stepped on.

- I should imagine, said Mariko.

- So he compromised with kneeling.

- Yes, it would be difficult to take an order while in full kowtow, she agreed.

- Even more difficult to fill an order in that position, laughed Saburo.

She threw back her head with abandon. Then:
Oh, I am having such a good time. You know how
to make a woman feel happy, Saburo-san.

- I have ways to make her feel even happier, he
said, drawing closer, nudging aside one of the
kneeling youths.

- Oh, so you do like girls after all then?

- Only during the rainy season, he said, his arm
around her, gripping. She once more threw back
her head.

15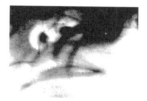

Mariko's famous throaty laugh again sounded
through the Yamato. Such an amusing person, she
said, addressing the two men seated in front of her.
Said he liked girls only during the rainy season. The
rainy season! Can you imagine?

More laughter. Hiroshi looked uncomfortable and
Paul looked puzzled. The two Japanese were entertaining the American in return for his having entertained them in return for their having entertained
him.

- Well, what have we here? asked Mariko as Midori and Emiko came bearing a wheel of brie, half a smoked sturgeon, a magnum of Moët & Chandon Brut Imperial and a box of Ritz.

Mariko sliced, spread, served, talking all the while. Took me to this most interesting place, she said. Traditional but contemporary. Oh, you would have liked it, Mr. Paul. Old Japan. Waiters in kimono but a computer at the cash desk. And expensive. I hesitate to think what the poor man must have spent on me.

- Poor man? Mr. Paul wanted to know.

- Friend of mine, said Hiroshi.

- Friend of *mine*, said Mariko. Then: So I got some valuable hints as to just what to do to the old Yamato here when I remodel.

- When is that? politely asked the foreigner.

- Well, before fall, I should think, said Mariko looking questioningly at Hiroshi.

When he did not respond, she said: Before - fall - I - should - think!

And when he yet again did not respond, she turned conversationally to Paul and said: Remember that girl we had here for you? You do? Well, there is just no apologizing for her. At any rate, I am so happy you didn't get on too well.

- Why?

- Because if you had it would have been just too

awful for you. She is not to be trusted, the little slut, and her a dyke and all. And not content with being a pervert she went and got a close friend of mine involved and it was all just disgusting, and I am thinking of just going to that degenerate place she works at and telling her employer about it.

- Why? asked Paul.

- Because this employer would become angry indeed if she knew that her little playmate was out with a man of all things, and one so much older, and her just out of high school herself.

- Oh, no, she continued, holding up a hand as though to forestall disagreement: You don't know lesbians. Terrible, they are. So jealous. Wouldn't be surprised if she actually killed the child in a fit of passion.

- Oh, really now, began Hiroshi in a tired voice.

- And who was it saw the evidence? cried Mariko. Who had her face rubbed into it? Oh, oh, oh! cried the apparently jealous woman, wagging her head. Then, upon seeing a guest enter: Oh, welcome, welcome. And over she tripped.

Mr. Paul wondered what the matter was.

- Women act a little funny when they get older, explained Hiroshi. Things yet plugged up.

- Oh, said Paul, apparently finding the observation reasonable. And who was Mitsuko-san with?

- Just guess, said Hiroshi, looking at the slowly liquefying brie.

- Yes, said Paul, then: You know? I think she likes you.

- I wish she didn't. This sort of thing makes Mariko impossible.

- Jealous?

- Yes, jealous.

- Me? Jealous? Of that little baggage? Humph! And Mariko, returning, snapped her fingers, then spread herself some sturgeon on Ritz. It is only the hurt of it, you see, dear Paul. I can call you my friend, can't I, even though you are a foreigner. It is the hurt of it, you see. Someone you loved, trusted. She dabbed an eye.

- Oh, really, said Hiroshi as though in disgust. And all I did was kiss the girl.

- There, you hear? He admits it. Shamelessly, he admits it. You have let the world know of it.

- You're the one doing all the shouting.

- I saw it. With-my-own-eyes.

This continued for a time, the girls looking on amused, the customers mystified. One had a good time at Miss Mariko's. You never knew what was going to happen with this fiery little lady.

Then there was another eruption. Oh, this rain. Here it is July. Will it never stop? Good Japanese though I am I cannot say that I find our rainy season attractive. My nerves - taut as piano wires, she added, thinking perhaps of that instrument at the Rat Mort.

- And there, look, a spot on the damask, another leak!

This exclamation had the desired effect of bringing the conversation back to the engrossing topic of renovations. And this time, Hiroshi, having learned his lesson, assented and agreed to almost every item mentioned.

16

- At least she has a place to renovate, said Mitsuko. Me, I have nothing at all. Only a position among female perverts.

She was perhaps suggesting that she might be set up in an establishment of her own. If so, Hiroshi either misunderstood or ignored.

Instead: Speaking of which, now she says she is going to go and tell the Mistress about us.

- But she doesn't even know her, snapped the girl.

- She will, sighed the man. She has her spies just everywhere.

- Well, what will I do? I'd lose my job if the Mistress ever thought I had gone out with a man, particularly to a love-hotel.

- The Colonial is not a love-hotel. It is a supper club.

- With beds, said Mitsuko scornfully, perhaps no longer feeling it profitable to simper and agree with just everything.

Hiroshi with dignity corrected: A single fold-out sofa . . .

- Is better than none, completed the waiter, an acned youth in a leather jacket with 'Kiss It' pricked in brilliants, as he swept away their pancakes.

- You do take me to strange places, said Hiroshi, looking around. The McDonald's-like hues were still there but the stuffed animals were not. Nor were the very young. Rather, the place was filled with insinuating young adults, mostly in leather, some in miniskirts, jeans, tank tops.

- It used to be called My Kitty. Now it is called My Pussy, volunteered Mitsuko. It caters to an older crowd now so that it can stay open later. Makes more money, she added.

- They ought to be home in bed, observed Hiroshi. Look at the time.

- It's not eleven yet. I should go back to Elle now though, I suppose. But I'm afraid to.

- Why not just quit, said Hiroshi, unthinking, then bit his lip.

- Whatever would I do for a living? she asked

instantly, looking at him hard.

- Well, there's always the Mistress, he said, lightly.

Mitsuko drew herself up. You imply that I am lesbian?

He laughed uneasily, then said: Sometimes I think they have it easier.

- Well, at least you have Madame Mariko. Me, I have no one.

Turning away Hiroshi joined two nearby girls in watching the barboy who stuck out his lips, half-opened his mouth and turned his cigarette end for end, the filter sticking out, the lit tip now inside his mouth.

- I wonder, he then said. She is never at the Yamato early anymore. Always out - always with Saburo.

The girls applauded. The bartender, pleased, attempted a smile, then suddenly started, spat, stuck out his tongue and began running about inside the bar. The girls, each of whom had 'Trés Chic' written over their right breasts, again clapped.

- And him your good friend, she said sympathetically, watching as the bartender drank glass after glass of water.

- Classmate, same university, same graduating class. And him a homo for all I know, he said.

- But, in that case you wouldn't have to worry, would you? she asked.

You never can tell, he said darkly. Then: That's a good trick if you can do it, he said, indicating the barboy, continuing with: Still, one expects a bit of gratitude in this life. It was me gave her the money for that place, you know. It was me that gave her her start in life, you know. It was me who picked her up out of nowhere and gave her this chance, you know.

He was becoming emotional but Mitsuko offered nothing in the way of solace. She merely regarding him with brilliant, expectant eyes, lips pursed, nodding as though she had somehow known all along.

After this she laid a hand on his arm and he looked at her gratefully and, while the jukebox bellowed its adolescent anguish, they spoke of other things.

17

Mariko looked around. The pews, the nave, the spotlighted chalice, the great plastic rose window, and nuns just everywhere.

- It won't last, she said.

- Oh, I don't know, said Saburo easily. You can't say it's not novel.

- That's just it. Too novel. We Japanese like our novelties, but they have to be familiar ones. This place is just too foreign.

And, as though proving her point, she pointed to the mother superior. Now what's that she asked.

- That's the madame. She's in charge, you see. That's why she carries the crucifix and has that scourge.

- Oh, no, cried Mariko. We Japanese like our little novelties but they ought be normal ones. This here is just, well, disgusting. All this foreign frippery.

A young nun approached, rosary rustling, and asked what they would have. Mariko regarded the menu, a simple parchment scroll. What on earth is a Communion Cocktail?

- You might try one, said Saburo roguishly: Make you forget your problems.

Organ music, 'Yesterday,' vox angelica, and Mariko continued: Just one of my problems is what I ought to do about that girl.

- Hiroshi's?

- Yes, her, the little viper

- Leave her alone. He'll forget about her soon enough.

- You don't know her. She's a crafty little thing.

Eyes like a snake, she has. And that hungry little
mouth.

- Speaking of hungry little mouths, I've got one
myself. And Saburo leaned forward, kissed Mariko
on the lips.

- Oh, you awful thing! she shrieked in merriment.
And in church like this, too!

After that she drank her Communion Cocktail
which seemed made of grenadine and Coca-Cola,
and he had an Angel's Tit which was crème de
cacao and Carnation Condensed Milk with a single
maraschino cherry on top.

Then Mariko turned in an animated manner and
said: Well, at least the rainy season seems over.

And they spoke of the weather for a time - still
humid, but perhaps it would be shortly fine -
before she reverted to her problem.

- Still, one has one's responsibilities, she said,
shooing away a nun who was attempting to bring
them something in a chalice. I really owe it to her,
you see, to correct her ways. She is yet a child. She
will in time be grateful.

- And how do you intend to correct her?

- Simply inform her employer, a somewhat severe
woman, I understand, and one who I have heard
takes an unseemly interest in young Mitsuko. I
think discipline will be meted out and accepted -
the poor thing has to keep her job, you see, having

thoughtlessly left my employment - and that will be the end of the matter. In no time she will, I imagine, lose what small taste for men she already has.

- Do women ever, asked Saburo sententiously, head cocked on one side, boyish smile in evidence.

The mother superior appeared with the bill.

- Here, let me see it. Mariko cast a practiced eye.

- Votive candles? What votive candles? We didn't order any votive candles.

The mother superior extended a mute hand toward their pew and there in a candelabra were burning a number.

- No, no, no! she said as Saburo paid the not inconsiderable bill. This place will not last. This is no way to do proper business.

18

Up the spiral staircase, chrome, one pair of sensible oxfords, one pair of high heels. At the top a burst of laser and the giant neon Titania bent down, touched the doorway with her magic wand, blinding with a blast of strobe.

- It's empty, said Sumire, staring.

- What? called back Mitsuko, deafened.

There seemed no one in the whole big strobe-lit, hi-tech place.

- They've gone somewhere else, cried Mitsuko, looking about.

- Who?

- The crowd that used to come here. This was the most popular discotheque in all of Akasaka.

- What happened? Sumire wanted to know.

- Nothing. It's just not the most popular anymore.

- Or popular at all, said Sumire, looking around at the emptiness. In the far distance a few youths chatted, trays in hands, but no one came to seat them so they sat themselves.

Sudden silence.

- Like lemmings, said Sumire, blinking her little eyes in wonderment.

- Yes, when the young take it into their heads to move they just do. So sudden, too. The management is always left gasping.

- The Titania's management must have fainted, said Sumire, marveling. The rent here's probably terrific.

- Oh, it will close soon, said Mitsuko. Nighttime business is like that. It has these sudden ups and downs.

- I just bet you're quoting your own Hiroshi-san, said Sumire knowingly, looking at her sensible shoes.

Mitsuko glanced at her friend: Not anymore. He is neglecting me shamelessly.

- For his Madame Mariko?

- No. And since she is neglecting *him* shamelessly, you'd think he'd have some time for me. He must be at a loose end nightly. So am I. That's why I asked you out.

Sumire received this with equanimity. Could we have a drink?

- No, it's impossible.

- But one is included in the entrance fee.

- I know, but one never gets one.

- Oh, said her friend, then: Poor Hiroshi-san. Where does he go when he's alone?

- How would I know, seeing how he's avoiding me.

- Excuse me, cried Sumire into the distance but not one of the chatting youths turned.

- See that corner? That is where Kawabata sat before he died, said Mitsuko.

- Ooh, spooky, was the rejoinder of her friend.

- Starlight Lounge. That is one of the places he goes to, said Mitsuko, answering the earlier question.

- Sophisticated, said Sumire, now herself just sophisticated enough to know.

- Oh, it is. I've been there. Just like a foreign country, Mitsuko repeated.

Sumire again shook an innocent head. She had never seen anything like that.

- I have never seen anything like that, she said.

- No reason why you should, was the unsympathetic rejoinder.

Sumire, mousey, looked up sharply: I have my ambitions as well, she said.

- Well, just keep them to yourself, said Mitsuko. My problem is what if Madame Mariko tells the Mistress.

- But you didn't do anything bad.

- You try to tell that to either of them. Awful women.

- Well, at least the rain's stopped, said Sumire, and after several more times attempting to attract the attentions of the distant waiters the two walked under the spent Titania and out into the warm summer night.

19

- Ugh, it is so hot, said Mariko. And no air conditioning.

- We just got here, said Hiroshi, unhappily. They probably only turn it on once the guest gets in. Saves energy.

- I would never save energy at the Yamato, said Mariko grandly. Then: You are certain it was this room?

- Yes, I guess so, said Hiroshi miserably.

- He guesses so? Did it mean so little to him? Has he forgotten then?

He wagged his head in despair. Mariko had insisted upon returning to what she referred to as the scene of the crime. Thus, they were in the room at the Colonial, supper on the way, Coolidge on the wall, and she was regarding the sofa, now folded out, as though it were bloodstained. The waiter wheeled in the food and began arranging it on the table.

- Will you please make the sofa go back in? said Hiroshi.

- Why? she asked.

- The servant, said Hiroshi in a low voice.

- Why? I will certainly never see him again, she answered loudly as the servant, unperturbed, set out the knives and forks, bowed, left.

- It just looks bad, said Hiroshi.

- Now he cares about how things look, said Mariko and did a nasty version of her famous throaty laugh. Then: What extraordinarily bad food—as always.

He bit into the steak and chewed a few times.

- But then they do not really have clientele at all

picky about the cuisine do they now? she asked.

Hiroshi chewed on, miserable.

- Really, the place has no tone, she said. I wonder you take here anyone you really cared about.

- We've been here often, as you know, and tonight you insisted.

I do not mean me. I meant her. The little viper. What is this?

- Mashed potatoes, he said, still chewing.

- Ah-ha, I thought so, she cried, as though in triumph, and pushed her plate away.

- Look, dear, why not just let bygones be bygones.

- But I saw it all. With-my-own-eyes. Right here. She indicated the steak, the salad, the mashed potatoes, the sofa.

Hiroshi looked as though he might yet again repeat that nothing had happened. Then, as though considering, said nothing, merely went on chewing that first bite.

- You look like a cow, she said suddenly, tittering. Chewing your cud, she added, giggling.

- It could be more tender, he said, ruefully.

- And so could you, said she.

Then, as he moved closer, taking advantage of this apparent change of mood: No, no, no. What do you think I am? In a place like this. That sofa. Still hot from your sin! And she convulsively jerked away causing the serving table to skitter off and bang against the wall.

- Oh, all over the floor, he said, groaning.

- It is only mashed potatoes, she said reassuringly. Then, looking more closely. And caramel custard. And then: Oh, I forgot to tell you.

Hiroshi flinched

- Very well, I won't. All right, I will. The Mistress came to see me last night while you were out with goodness knows whom. She just made a short professional call. What a cold woman, too.

- What did she want?

- Nothing I didn't expect. Says you are taking up too much of the child's time, creating a bad precedent, that the other girls are gossiping, her going out with a man and all, wants to make you stop, for appearance's sake, wants me to use what small influence I may yet have with you.

Hiroshi stared at her, then: Mariko, you are lying.

- Well, really, she cried. As though my humiliations were not already enough, with the whole world knowing of your going behind my back.

- Mariko, you are lying, he said.

She flung out her hands, slammed the console.

- And this is the thanks I get, then. After I showed that woman the door, said that it was no concern of mine if she could not look after her little girlfriends, after I had saved-your-face. Wa! And she burst into apparent tears.

The servant appeared.

- What do you want? she screamed.

He indicated the small red light.

- You banged the button, said Hiroshi.

While the servant, who had seen everything while working there, mopped up the mashed potatoes, Mariko continued with: And that is the thanks I get for attempting to save your honor.

The servant departed and, after glancing to ascertain the postion, Mariko impetuously threw herself on the sofa, sobs now muffled.

Hiroshi joined her, and after they had made up, after she had found her stockings and he his jockey shorts, flung into the crème caramel which the servant had neglected to mop up - after all of this, she sat at the small pull-out vanity and repaired her face.

- And how is Saburo? asked Hiroshi perhaps thinking it of some advantage to appear jealous as well.

- No, no, no, cried Mariko merrily: I will not have you jealous. There is nothing like that at all. After all, he is your blessed classmate. We are just good friends, he and I. He takes me about when you neglect me. That is all. Interesting places.

- Like homo bars, said Hiroshi, as though bitter.

- Well, after all, he owns one. But, let me tell

you, Watanabe-san, that man is no homo. And she went off into her famous laughter as he sponged the crème caramel off his underpants.

- And do put something around you. You look too grotesque sitting there like that. What's this?

She pushed the button, then pushed again. The sofa did not budge.

- I do believe it's broken, she said.

20

- At any rate, she said that the Mistress came to see her and said you shouldn't see me.

- This doesn't seem very likely, said Mitsuko sipping her Chivas, nibbling her Ritz. How would she even know her?

- These people all seem to know each other, said Hiroshi shaking his head. But how would the Mistress know about us? Did you tell her anything?

- Me? asked Mitsuko, her fingers splayed against her chest as though in surprise. Of course not.

- Well, when people get intimate they tell secrets.

- Look! Me and the Mistress are not intimate.

- Well, it's a big mystery, he said, sighing, downing his Chivas.

- Yes, as well it might be because she is-making-the-whole-thing-up.

- No, no, no. Mariko may be a bit difficult some-times, but she never lies.

- She lies all the time, was Mitsuko's opinion as she speared a kiwi. People can see who they want, she added, irrelevant.

- She is seeing too much of Saburo if you ask me, said Hiroshi. Maybe I ought to go and tell on them.

- Who would you tell? Unlike poor me, they have no employer. They are the self-employed - fortu-nate folk that they are.

- Well, said Hiroshi.

- People can see who they want, repeated Mitsuko, her voice rising.

- Absolutely right, said Ken, flashing perfect teeth, touching his perm, bending over them with: Perhaps if not myself, though I am at your service (here a mock little bow) perhaps Jun or Joji here. He indicated the two affable, dressed-up youths.

- Where is Minoru? asked Hiroshi. I thought he was master here.

- Who, please? asked Ken, as though failing to comprehend. Then: Oh, Minoru-san, you mean? Yes, I do believe he was here for a time.

- Just last month, said Hiroshi. And you were sitting over there, neglected.

Ken gave a brilliant smile. Well, life has its ups and downs. In any event, I am now the master of the Empire. At your service. Again, the irritating little bow.

Then: You were interested in Minoru? I am afraid I must tell you that our young men here are all one-hundred-percent-straight and, in any event, we do not allow them to go out with male customers. Then, to Mitsuko: We have such trouble with homos, you see. They are not satisfied to be with their own kind.

- I'm no homo! shouted Hiroshi and an older woman, much dressed up, turned to stare from a table loaded with exotic fruit and several young men in sharkskin. Angry, he downed his Chivas.

- In that case, I beg your pardon, said Ken instantly with his little bow. It takes all kinds to make the world go round. Then, to Mitsuko: Jun, here? Joji, there? Perhaps myself?

The girl hesitated as though among flavors, then said: Nothing right now, thank you. I'll just talk with my friend.

- Really, fumed Hiroshi, that little whore.

- Oh, no, said Mitsuko. He told you they were all one-hundred-percent-straight.

- I was speaking metaphorically, and a man can be

a whore just as much as a woman can. It's all a question of money.

Then, considering what he had said: Now don't get me wrong.

- You're saying that if you put up the money for me to open my own place it would make me a whore!

- I am saying nothing of the sort. It would be a business deal.

Silence. Then, upon further consideration: Not that I could possibly afford to do anything like that. I have learned my lesson. Never again.

- Oh, why did you ever bring me to this awful place, complained Mitsuko as though near tears.

- But you asked to come here, he said, his voice rising. You said you wanted to see how the other half lived. I didn't want to bring you. I hate this place! All these little permed-up kept boys primping away! Only reason we're here at all is because Mariko doesn't have her spies here. Yet, maybe, he shouted.

Two other patrons, ample women in flowered prints, stared. One of them dropped her mango.

- Hiroshi-san, you've had too much Chivas, said Mitsuko, pulling his sleeve.

- I don't care! he shouted.

Ken approached, bent over Mitsuko, whispered.

- They want you to keep your voice down.

- Keep my voice down? I'll keep my voice down, I will!

He downed another Chivas straight. Who they think they are. Little whores! They can't tell me keep my voice down.

Then as several of the boys moved in and began flailing: Hey! What you doing anyway. Wa!

21

- Kicked out of the Empire, drunk. How disgusting. Yes, Minoru heard all about it from one of those little boy whores who work there. Minoru? Why, of course. He works for me now. I am going to put him in full kimono when I redo the Yamato. He will look divine kneeling and bowing there when my patrons arrive.

- In the foyer? asked Hiroshi looking at the Louis Quinze.

- We're going to call it the genkan again. But don't change the subject. Who was that girl you were with? No one there knew her.

Hiroshi's face showed a certain relief. Oh, friend

of my wife's. Widow. Lonely. Heard about the place but first time and all, so I took her.

- Very kind, said Mariko coldly. Just as long as it wasn't her.

- Her?

- The little viper.

- Oh, the little viper? Oh, no. Ha-ha. Don't see much of her anymore. She's off with her, ha-ha, girlfriends.

- She still at the dyke bar?

- Guess so.

- You were so drunk. Must have had a real hangover next day.

Hiroshi looked carefully rueful, mindfully hung his head. Mariko tittered.

- Little head still hurting? she asked.

He nodded, apparently miserable.

- Well, I cannot do anything for you tonight, my dear, she said, spreading the folds of a light summer wrap. Saburo is taking me out again. Really, so attentive he is, Saburo. Oh, you thought we might go out, just you and me? Why ever didn't you say so? Earlier. I do tend to get booked up a bit these days.

Then, in answer to his complaint: Me? Seeing too much of Saburo? Well, really. This is a bit much, if you ask me. Isn't it you who are seeing a bit much of someone else? And I do not mean your wife's lonesome widow friend. You're a fine one to talk.

She glanced around the Yamato, glared at Midori who slank back into the kitchen.

- Really! she opined. Then: At least he's a gentleman. He doesn't get himself kicked out of host clubs by boy whores! Oh, ha-ha, I would like to have seen that. Then: Like my new wrap? Cardin. Original. Got it at Mitsukoshi.

- Then it can't be too original.

- I mean the design is original, not the actual wrap itself. So smart it is. He's taking me out to the Starlight Lounge. How did he know about it? Well, really, you don't own it, you know. Anyway, I told him about it, that's how. Really, you are so small-minded. No wonder you get kicked out of places.

Then, apparently thinking of the warm weather and her Cardin wrap: I wonder if this is too much.

22

- Speaking of cocks, I saw Ken Takakura's.
- Wherever?
- At the gym. I go there every day to work out.

Not dressed like this, of course. And he was in the shower.

- How was it?

- Oh, nice. They have it all fixed up. Private units, sting-spray.

- No, no. The cock.

- Well, ordinary, of course.

- Then what's all the fuss? asked the bartender who had been listening. Why are you talking about it?

- But, I've seen him so often up there on the screen, was the answer. And it is very interesting to see someone's cock after you have seen him so often up there on the screen.

Hiroshi, who had also been listening, turned away from the two with a grimace. He apparently did not enjoy being in the Lovely Boy though it was, everyone agreed, one of its better nights. Friday, payday, a warm clear evening, AIDS (for the time being perhaps) forgotten. And in any event, the Lovely Boy had a plaque on the door firmly repulsing foreigners. No Foreigners, it said.

Though preventing unclean infections from abroad was only one of the reasons, Saburo had already confided. It's just that we're sort of like a club here, he'd said. And a new face barging in, a different-colored one at that, sort of shreds the social fabric, as it were.

The social fabric was at present all of a piece.

Boys, lovely and otherwise, pressed against - among others - Hiroshi sitting sullen on his stool. And men more or less Hiroshi's age, company lapel-pins in their pockets, were pressing back. On the hi-fi Judy Garland sang her heart out.

The bartender bowed and Saburo slid onto the stool beside Hiroshi's. Sorry, he said, just checking the week's receipts.

- Satisfactory I would say, judging from all the activity, said Hiroshi dryly.

- Yes, can't complain. Things are looking up. Course it's payday. Anyway, since we get all our money on turnover, the more the better.

- Actually, I wanted to talk to you, said Hiroshi.

- Talk away then, said Saburo with a smile.

- Here?

- Well, it's good business to show my face here once in a while. Makes them feel at home to see the owner about. Hi, there, long time no see! And he smiled and winked at someone behind Hiroshi.

- Got a pretty good mix here now if I do say so. These kids all have this liking for middle-aged guys. And these middle-aged guys all like kids. It seems to work. Funny tastes people have. Good looking boys just out of high school and they take a shine to someone short and forty or so with a little pot-belly and a receding hairline.

As he said this a good looking boy, seemingly just

out of high school, looked Hiroshi straight in the eye, smiled, and asked if he would please pass the toothpicks.

Hiroshi glared, did so, and Saburo chuckled. Barbra Streisand took over.

- Well, what did you want to talk about, old friend? asked Saburo leaning back against the bar, regarding the busy clientele.

- Look, did Mariko say anything about Mitsuko?

- No, nothing, not a thing, not at all, lied his old friend.

- I'm a bit worried, you see. And you seem to be seeing her more than I am these days.

- Lovely person, Mariko. Always a pleasure.

- She is threatening things if I don't stop seeing Mitsuko, said Hiroshi, emotionally.

- Now, now, said his old classmate.

- I do think that's common, said a voice beside them: Why does that kind always use girls' names.

- Mitsuko, indeed. If he feels that way about his boyfriend he ought to put him in drag too.

- Now just you look here! said Hiroshi, roused.

- That's all right, that's all right, said Saburo. No offense meant nor taken, I'm sure. And you, old pal, you better behave.

- What about that faggot there? He just called me a faggot.

Voices now rose above that of Barbra Streisand

until with many a smile and chuckle Saburo made peace.

- Look, old buddy, he then said, straight into Hiroshi's ear: This is my bread-and-butter. I know you're not queer and that should be enough.

Hiroshi looked around. Posters of Dietrich in pants, Dean in jeans; pictures of pre-teen boy singers with dimples; guests with small bangles and swiveling eyes: the high laughter and the steady clang of the old-fashioned American cash register. He sighed.

After that they talked on and finally Hiroshi came to, perhaps, the point : So, you see, since it's inadvisable for me to see Mitsuko myself - she's come to expect too much and then there is Mariko to watch out for - I was wondering if you would, well, take her out from time to time

- Me? Mitsuko? asked Saburo with what appeared to be genuine surprise.

- Yes. You could let her know that I am going to have to back off for a little while, until things cool down, you might say. And you could sort of get her out of the idea too that I am going to get her her own place, if you don't mind.

- *I'm* certainly not getting her her own place, said Saburo.

- I know, I know. It's just to keep her occupied, your seeing her, I mean.

- Well, I don't know about that, said Saburo with

what appeared reluctance

- Please, for my sake, said Hiroshi, again emotional.

More heads turned, more glances shot. This time there was a murmur of approbation among the nearby clientele. The bartender beamed, apparently approving of what he perhaps took for middle-aged love.

Then the nearby suspended conversation was continued: Talking about famous cocks, did I ever tell you what this older friend of mine told me about Mishima's?

But this information went unheard by Hiroshi. He and Saburo were busy planning together how to arrange the meeting with Mitsuko - how to make it seem casual, natural, normal.

23

- Wa! Tanaka-san! Imagine meeting you here of all places. It's been a long time. Now you just sit down with us for a bit. This is my old friend, Saburo Tanaka, and this is Mitsuko Koyama, and, well, it certainly has been a long time.

In the background 'Don't Get Around Much Anymore' was once more heard, Saburo smiled his boyish best, and sat down at their table, just as though the meeting was accidental and had not been several times rehearsed.

- Funny thing, I was just talking to Mitsuko here about you, what a good friend you've been to me, Old Classmate, and there you appeared. Then: Didn't know you came here much.

-Don't get around much anymore, said Saburo with a lazy smile at Mitsuko. But I still manage to hit the old Starlight Lounge.

- I love it here, she proffered: Just like a foreign land.

- It never changes in this world of change, said Hiroshi seriously. And that is one of the things to appreciate about it.

The two then went on eating their chicken à la king while Saburo had a brandy and Hiroshi continued with: Like the cuisine.

- Umm, delicious, was the opinion of Mitsuko: Just like a foreign land.

Then Hiroshi held a finger in the air as though testing the wind and, on cue, the headwaiter glided over and whispered into his ear, and Hiroshi assumed an expression of surprise, wondered who on earth could have known he was here, and went off to answer what was assumed to be the telephone.

During the interval, Saburo deployed himself to

be as charming as possible and Hiroshi returned to find the two in laughter. Oh, your friend, she gasped: He is so humorous.

Hiroshi nodded, as though preoccupied, then said: Look, there is no apologizing for this. Head office. Emergency. I've got to run. Mitsuko, shall I take you home? Not that I have time to. No, I have an idea. It is very rude of me but might I ask my friend Saburo here to take you out a bit? You don't mind, do you? I thought not. And, Mitsuko-san, I'll be in touch.

And he raced from the Starlight Lounge while Satch (Happy) Suzuki looked after him with what appeared to be disappointment.

- Well, said Mitsuko. Just like that.

- Yes, said Saburo easily. He always was a bit strange, even in school.

- Impossibie to imagine him as a schoolboy, was her opinion.

- Should think not, he said, smiling: You're still quite a schoolgirl yourself.

- I am eighteen, she said, as though this was a virtue.

Then: Head office, she said. Humph! President Mariko I should imagine.

- She is an unusual woman, was his opinion.

- Isn't she though, said Mitsuko. I understand she is a friend of yours as well.

- Yes, family friend as it were, old friend of

Hiroshi-san's that she is, you see.

- I see, said Mitsuko as though she saw nothing. Then. She seems to take very good care of him. Possessive, you might say.

- Yes, you might say that, he said reasonably. Then: You see, his is the type of personality that seems to demand that. There is something child-like about him, don't you think?

- Yes, she said, turning and looking, smiling as though she was finally with a real adult. I do think so. Now that you mention it.

They talked on to the strains of 'Chattanooga Choo-Choo' and the coffee and apple pie and brandy were all finished at the same time. Then Saburo produced the money Hiroshi had forced on him, paid the bill, tipped the headwaiter, and hand-ed a small bank note to the happy Satch (Happy) Suzuki as they left.

24

- And then he took me to this wonderful place, all flowers, where the boys kneel at you, and real

TV stars sometimes come, though none happened to be there then.

- And did he kiss you? Sumire wanted to know.

- No, not yet, they're classmates after all, Mitsuko answered, dodging the swinging leather jacket of a large, adult, shaved-head male. My Pussy is getting very tough, she observed.

- Police came in day before yesterday, offered Sumire, making faces over her Johnny Walker over Lady Borden.

- Were you here?

- No, just I heard, TV. Anyway, go on.

- Well, anyway, said Mitsuko reverting: Not that I would mind at all.

- I should think not. Being kissed by a stranger, imagine. I've only been kissed by my mother so far.

- Would not have minded at all, repeated Mitsuko. But he was too much of a gentleman even to attempt it. Put me in a taxi with that boyish little smile of his.

- Is he really so dreamy?

- Dreamy.

- More so than Hiroshi Watanabe?

- Oh, him. He's not dreamy at all.

- But aren't they of an age? asked Sumire.

- Age is not all that matters, said Mitsuko mysteriously, then dodged as two young males, drunk, crashed into the next table, collapsed. Outside motorbikes revved endlessly and all of Harajuku swaggered past.

- My Pussy is getting dangerous, observed Sumire.

- Yes, we probably shouldn't come anymore.

- It can't last, was Mitsuko's friend's opinion. Not when it gets as open as this. The police will tolerate anything but openness. They'll be doing drugs here next, you know.

A large drunken youth at the next table produced a bottle of pills, poured them down his throat, and then drank water from a pitcher, one with a mother cat and her young on it, relic from the days of My Kitty.

- See? Then: Well, you going to let him take you out again?

- I might, said Mitsuko. If he asks. What with Hiroshi-san permanently out of the picture and all.

- Permanently? small eyes bright, asked Sumire as though this news had a special interest for her.

- Take him, take him, said Mitsuko easily. But, really, he's more trouble than he's worth.

- Isn't it Madame Mariko who's the real trouble?

- Yes, he's just her slave.

- Slave, repeated Sumire, marveling.

- You girls into that? asked the acned waiter, now crew-cut and tattooed, as he swept away their plates. Why don't you let me introduce you to someone I happen to know?

- Why don't you mind your own business? said Mitsuko. Then to her friend: This place has had it.

- Hasn't it just. Go on.

- Well, as I say, seeing as how Hiroshi-san is neglecting me, I just don't see any reason why I can't go out with Saburo-san. If he should happen to ask me, that is.

- Is he a company president too?

- No, he's not.

- What does he do then?

- Well - promise not to laugh - he's the sole owner and proprietor of this very successful bar.

- What's to laugh at?

- Well, you see, one of the reasons it is so successful is that it is for men only.

- Oh, no, Sumire, laughing.

- You promised not to laugh, said Mitsuko.

- Not another gay bar. Really, Mitsuko-san, you seem to collect them, and you work in one of them.

- That's a lesbian bar.

- Same thing, was her friend's opinion.

- Saburo-san's is a cut well above the others and, as I say, he's in it only for the money. Homosexuality is one of Japan's major growth industries, he says.

- Oh, really? asked Sumire, perhaps impressed. Then, as though remembering: Speaking of which, did Madame Mariko go tell the Mistress about you and Hiroshi-san like you were afraid she'd done?

- It is difficult to say, said Mitsuko. Probably not. The Mistress has been more friendly lately. Frankly, I am a little disturbed. She cries now. Makes these scenes in the kitchen. Calls me stone-hearted.

- Really? I feel sorry for her, said the soft-hearted Sumire. There's this scene in 'A Mother's Heart' -

- Sorry? For her? asked Mitsuko. She's awful. Has this thing about the ocean, always got Charles Trenet's 'La Mer' on. Says it calls her, will claim her yet. And so when she feels this way she starts talking about a watery death and then goes and locks herself in the bathroom.

- Down the drain, laughed Sumire merrily, then, remembering to be sorry: Poor thing.

- You know, I wouldn't mind putting up with her, frankly, but it is this awful possession I don't like. I think that jealousy is a very vulgar emotion.

- Like Madame Mariko's for poor Hiroshi-san, said Sumire quickly.

Mitsuko looked her approval: Precisely. Then: Look at me, I don't feel possessive about poor Hiroshi-san.

- No, not when you have someone as interesting as your Saburo-san, said Sumire with what appeared to be envy.

- Well, we will just have to wait and see, said Mitsuko with apparent satisfaction.

Then the tattooed youth brought a bottle of vodka and four glasses and said that it was compliments of the gentlemen there, indicating the next table where two big boys, one pierced, one tattooed, sat and stared, and Mitsuko pulled Sumire to her feet and together the two fled My Pussy and ran out into the hot, humid, July night.

25

- Jealous? Me? Jealous? cried Mariko. No, not at all. It's just that he never calls me anymore and now I hear he's taking out that lesbian hussy of yours!

- Don't, my dear, said Hiroshi, wiping his brow. Not on top of this heat.

- I suppose it's my fault that the air conditioning broke down, tonight of all nights, payday and the hottest July on record said the seven o'clock report.

They were sitting wilting in the Yamato. A few of the girls were in the corners, fanning, panting, Midori with a wide wet patch.

- Women who sweat, said Mariko reproachfully, staring.

- Surely we all do that, said Hiroshi, closing his eyes.

- But so visibly. I never do that.

He opened his eyes, looked, affirmed: You're right.

- See? Then, it being too hot to argue: Neglected that's what I am.

- I'm not neglecting you. I am right here. As always.

- I didn't mean you. Really, what could he see in the little viper anyway.

- I am sure I don't know, said Hiroshi virtuously.

- Well, what did you see in her, then?

- Me? Oh, I don't know. The promise of youth, I suppose. Something romantic. Something silly.

This display of honesty was rewarded with a pat on the cheek. Poor old Hiroshi-san, she said, smiling: Getting on, aren't you.

- I am not alone in that, he said, looking at her, and this impertinence was rewarded with a further pat, one more of a slap.

- I do wish those repairmen would hurry. They said they would come right over.

- Service isn't what it used to be, said Hiroshi, perhaps quoting. Then, as though a thought had just struck: What are you going to do if the Yamato goes all Old Japan? Old Japan had no air conditioning.

- Electric fans, said Mariko at once.

- Old Japan did not have those either.

- All right, what did Old Japan have then?

- Nothing. Just the natural breezes.

- What natural breezes? Down in this basement?

- Perhaps Old Japan is not such a good idea, he then said, as though this was the conclusion toward which the conversation had been leading.

- No, said Mariko adamant. We can put up with a bit of inconvenience if it means getting back to our roots.

- I should hardly call putting in a few tatami getting back to our roots, said Hiroshi.

- No, but it's a beginning. And no heaters in the winter either.

- Just a little charcoal, said Hiroshi with a small smile. But no electric lights.

- Just candles, said Mariko with a little laugh. And no running water.

- Just a bucket, said Hiroshi, laughing. And no flush toilets.

- Just an open drain! cried Mariko with a shriek. Oh, ha-ha-ha, how amusing you are, Hiroshi-san. Oh, what would I ever do without you?

- Well, here I am, he said simply.

This last remark, however, seemed not taken as intended for Mariko looked darkly at him, reminded perhaps of someone who was not there. She bit a nail.

- I simply don't see what he sees in her. Tell me, frankly. Is she that good in bed?

He made his eyes round, his mouth to match. How would I know?

- You forget, she said: I saw.

- You saw before I had the opportunity to find out, he said, as though exasperated.

This Mariko disregarded: She takes all my friends. First you, then him. Goodness knows who is next.

- Have you any more friends?

- She's insatiable. She's even taken out that foreign friend of yours, even. And you ought to do something about that Saburo. After all, he's your classmate.

At which Hiroshi looked imploringly at the ceiling, then folded his hands and together they sat in the heat awaiting the repairman.

26

- I thought it might be another of those bars again, said Paul, looking at all the girls. You like odd places.

- I am doing research. You see, if I am going to open up a place of my own I have to know a lot about the business.

- Is that what you are going to do?

- Well, maybe. It all depends.

He swiveled on his stool to face her and a passing young woman, bangs and fringes, banged into his shoulder, then said: Watch it!

Paul stared after the wide-shouldered retreating figure, then turned to Mitsuko: What kind of place have you taken me to this time?

- A brand-new concept.

- I see, he said, rubbing his shoulder.

- The Elle is old-fashioned, all long skirts and stuffed animals and music boxes. The Gambling Girl here is modern, all leather and heavy metal. I understand we have to stand up in the ladies.

- Is that possible? he wanted to know.

- Yes, she said as though considering: It's . . . possible.

An older young lady, crew-cut with safety-pin earrings, was regarding Paul with a steady hatred. Is it safe here? he wondered, nervous.

- Yes, as long as you are with a girl. If you came in alone, though, they might work you over. And if you were a Japanese man it would be even worse.

- You want to run this kind of bar?

- Nothing this advanced, perhaps, but something

this unusual, I think.

- How about an old-fashioned bar for men and women?

She shook her head: Far out, she said, then: I've got this friend who is quite successful in the business and he says that homosexuality is the growth industry in Japan.

Sound of motorcycles roaring to a stop, then into the Gambling Girl stomped three more customers.

- You see, said Mitsuko with approval. The place is catching on. Then, as though reminded of why she had asked the foreigner out: I wanted to talk with you. It's about this possible patron.

- Hiroshi-san.

- Precisely. You see he has been neglecting me recently and I just have to know if he is sufficiently interested in helping me with my career or not. Because if not I have this other possibility that I might be cultivating, you see. But since I met the first one first it would be only fair to give him the benefit of our longer acquaintance. No, no, I am here with my friend. We are talking, she said, this last to a large, booted young woman who had taken her arm.

- Well, continued Paul, staring at the intruder, who stared back: What do you want me to do?

- I want you to find out if he is that interested.

- Why don't you come with me? I'll show you who's interested, said the large young person.

- No, no, said Mitsuko, disengaging herself.

- I suppose you're used to this, said Paul.

- Well, at the Elle it's a little less direct. No, no. Please!

She moved to the other side of Paul and said: Would you?

- Well, yes, I'll ask.

- And a foreign man at that, said the large young woman shaking her heavy head and staring.

- Are you done studying? asked Paul nervously. I think we'd better go.

- Perhaps you're right. I don't think actually I'll be thinking of opening anything quite as advanced as this.

As they turned to leave, a number of the young women lounging at the bar, legs outstretched, whistled at Mitsuko and one slapped Paul on the rump.

Outside, he ruefully rubbed and looked up at the sign, a young person on a motorcycle in neon. Where do these women come from? he wondered.

- Oh, you know, sales girls, bank clerks, kindergarten teachers on their day off, said Mitsuko knowledgeably.

27

- Girls really like to be made a fuss over, said Saburo, indicating the kneeling youth.

- It makes me feel like a princess in Old Japan, said Mitsuko, verifying his prescience. And him in full kimono and all, she added. Don't they worry about creasing?

- Not to worry is part of the charm, said Saburo. If he fussed about a crease the customer might feel slighted.

- That's true, said Mitsuko, nodding. Then: You know so much, Mr. Saburo. Are there any places where the girls bow and scrape like this?

- Only in the lower-class establishments, oddly enough.

- Well, this place is not low-class, said Mitsuko looking about at the minor TV personalities and the single ex-movie-star.

- Not at all, and I would hate for you to see the bill.

She giggled, delighted, then asked: Does he stay there all evening, one for each couple?

- Oh, no. He's waiting for our order.

After they had ordered, they continued talking

about business. There is this place called Hometown, he said. It's all gotten up rustic with real farm boys in workcoats and loincloths and the girls come in after work and eat mountain ferns and sweet potatoes and make dates.

- With each other? Mitsuko wanted to know.

Saburo laughed his boyish laugh. No, no - hey, you been working at that place too long - no, they take the boys out afterward, feed them and then off to some motel somewhere. All these girls got cars.

- Do they pay the establishment?

- Don't have to. You should see how much mountain fern costs.

- Do they pay the farmboys?

- At their discretion. Usually the lads are too shy to ask.

- It doesn't sound that attractive, was Mitsuko's opinion.

- To a certain kind of person, said Saburo thoughtfully. Look, these poor girls have been taking guff all day long from their boss or their principal or their manager or someone. They want to let off some steam, as it were. So they come to the Hometown and here they are, like back where they came from, only now they got the money, the car, the power. And there, standing in front of them, are young examples of the oppressor. Do you blame them?

- No, I guess not.

- Oh, I've been there. Friend of mine runs it. Does quite well. Those girls talk awful. They call the boys turds and worse.

- My!

- And order them out after work - feed them, finger them and . . . well, I guess you can figure out the rest.

Mitsuko looked at the Foujita and seemed to be thinking. Well, she finally said: I just do not believe that I could rape a man like that.

- Well, as I'm saying, it takes a special kind of young lady. Then: There's only one drawback, my friend tells me.

- What could that be?

- The boys don't last. Some of them are enthusiastic about the job at first, but little by little, they get pale and weak and then have to go back to their own hometowns. Attrition.

- And supply falls below demand.

- Hey, you got a little business head on your shoulders.

- Well, you see, I'm thinking perhaps of starting up a little place of my own. Oh, nothing like Hometown, but nothing like Elle either.

- I agree. Nothing too kinky ever lasts long in our society.

- I was thinking of just some place where boys

and girls could just be friendly with each other.

- Be quite a novelty, said Saburo seriously but then asked nothing more about Mitsuko's proposed place, perhaps realizing that its financing was as yet undetermined.

- All these places here, she continued, meaning, apparently, Tokyo: And all of them simply designed to make money out of people's desires.

- Hey, you're quite the little philosopher, said Saburo. But that, after all, is the basis of all commerce. You only buy what you want. So the seller must bring about this want, even if it is not already there.

- Yes, look at the Yamato, said Mitsuko with sudden fierceness. Madame Mariko just has those girls showing themselves off shamelessly. They are all but falling out of their dresses. It's disgusting. Like a meat market . One of them, I saw it with my own eyes, was bulging out of her zipper.

- Hey, he said with his little laugh. Go easy there.

- I worked there, I know. I saw how she operates. Shameless it is. If I thought that I would ever turn into a person like her, well, I just wouldn't go into the business.

Then she stopped, appeared contrite, said: Oh, I'm so sorry, I had forgotten that she was a friend of yours, that you had been seeing something of her lately.

Having apparently forgotten nothing of the sort
she now sat and awaited his reply, waving aside a
crouched youth offering pistachios.

- Well, yes. You see, she's an old friend of
Hiroshi's and I'm an old friend of his, you see. But,
often? Not nowadays. No, I wouldn't say that.
Drink up.

He motioned to a young man who scurried over.

- Maybe I'll put my foot on his neck, she said, giggling.

- I'd rather you put it on mine, said Saburo with a
fond glance. And they laughed long and loud while
the kneeling youth waited.

28

Mariko looked around. The pillars, the candles,
the plastic lotuses, the Buddhist altar, and nuns just
everywhere.

- It was all different last time. Christian, she said.
Then: Well, this won't last either.

- Oh, I don't know, said Hiroshi easily. You can't
say it's not a novelty.

- That's the problem. We Japanese like our novelties but they can't be too familiar. This is a Buddhist temple. We've avoided them since childhood. The place is just too Japanese. There, just look at that.

A Buddhist priest, brocade and headdress, approached, produced a lacquered sutra-case inside which was the menu.

- What on earth is a Pure Land Fizz? she wanted to know.

- Might try one.

- I think I just will, said Mariko. Then they sat and listened to the tape of monks chanting away and she sneezed once or twice at all the incense.

- A church, eh? he asked.

- Cathedral. Ah-choo. But it didn't last.

- I suppose it was Saburo-san who introduced you to such an interesting place.

-Yes, as a matter of fact. He knows how to take a person out.

- Meaning that I don't? Well, I would never have chosen this place. And it was you who brought me here, don't forget. Won't last. Imagine putting money in a place like this. All gloom and smoke and gongs. Too bad it wasn't him you could bring to show the change to.

She glanced briefly at him, then said: Well, there is apparently a reason. The little viper's got him.

- No! said Hiroshi as though surprised.

- Yes. My people tell me he's taken her out quite a few times and at least once to that lovely place where the men are all over the floor that he took me to that I liked so much. Ugh!

- What's the matter?

- This. The Pure Land Fiz seemed made mainly of grenadine and Coca-Cola. She put it firmly on the sutra-stand behind which they were seated and said: Seriously, I am thinking of complaining.

- To whom? About what? I didn't do anything.

She briefly pressed his hand. I know, dear. You're true-blue. Right now. No, I am thinking of reporting that menace to the Mistress of the Elle. That your Mitsuko is seeing too much of Master Saburo. And besides, you see, it looks so odd: lesbian bar girl going out with gay bar master. She will appreciate that point.

- I wouldn't do that, he said mildly.

- I know you wouldn't, she said: That is why I am forced to take steps. You don't care how I feel - humiliated.

- But -

- First she attempts to poison you against me and now she is turning him against me, Saburo-san - your classmate, she flung accusingly.

- Well, you wouldn't know it these days, would you, was the unexpectedly sarcastic reply: You'd really think that Saburo-san was your classmate the way you carry on.

- You say that! To me! And it was you who drove me into his arms. Drove me. By carrying on with that little viper. I sought understanding. Someone to talk to. And now you accuse me of unspeakable things.

- Unspeakable things? he said, voice rising: As though being a classmate was unspeakable. Really! You women, you just don't understand what a sacred bond between men being classmates is. It is a very important relationship. Perhaps the strongest that a Japanese man can have, and I will not have it sullied.

His voice had been steadily rising and now the head priest hurried up, one finger to his lips, the other hand making soothing gestures. Then, his purpose accomplished, both Hiroshi and Mariko contrite in the face of what seemed real ecclesiastical authority, he smiled and indicated the altar.

With the roar of a struck gong the floor show began. Two nuns loosened their habits and then simulated an act of love, assisted by various of the Buddhist implements lying about.

- Your little friend ought to be here, said Mariko bitter. But Hiroshi was gazing at the writhing floor show and did not answer. So, after the girls with many an obeisance had retired and resumed their habits, Mariko looked around and said: What a dump. It is not going to work, I can just feel it, lesbian acts or not. Let's get out of here.

When the head priest brought the bill Mariko cast a practiced eye, then exclaimed: Holy candles? What holy candles? We didn't use any holy candles!

The priest extended a mute hand toward the flaming altar, illuminating the Buddha.

- No, no, no, she said as Hiroshi paid the very large bill. This place won't last, this is no way to do business.

- Yes, said Hiroshi, pocketing his wallet, agreeing: Too Japanese, he added, as though hopefully seeing his opportunity: Things Japanese simply won't sell.

- Nonsense, said Mariko as the great temple doors closed behind them: It's all in how you do it.

29

Mitsuko toyed with her chicken à la king, looked languidly at Tokyo twinkling below.

- It's the heat, Hiroshi said, guessing.

- It's nothing of the sort. This place is fully air-conditioned, she said, turning to him. It's just that I am remembering the first time you took me here. How full of life and enthusiasm I was. How young.

- It has only been a month or so. You cannot have so aged in that time.

- Perhaps not, she said wearily, but I feel that I have. I have had much experience. Being neglected, for example.

- Oh, that, said Hiroshi as though everything were now explained. I have told you, you know, that it is better for the time being not to be too much seen together. You have your career to think of.

- Humph! Mitsuko seemed to have a low opinion of her career so far. And I had such dreams, she stated.

As though he knew of just what such dreams consisted, Hiroshi displayed concern, rather, at her lack of appetite: You are not eating, he said.

- The heat.

- There. Just as I said.

This continued for a while as the band played its limited repertoire. Then Mitsuko got around to perhaps what she really wanted to talk about. About your friend, she said.

- Which one? he wanted to know, candid, eyes bright.

- Tanaka-san.

- Oh, Saburo. And a good friend he is too. We're classmates, you know.

- I know. I've been seeing something of him.

- Have you now? he said easily. Well he's a steadying influence.

- We've been getting close, she said, staring, as though to judge the effect.

- How close? asked Hiroshi with less easy a manner

- Pretty, she said with satisfaction.

- Oh, well, he said light, false: How close can you get with a homo?

She affected dismay. Really, you slander your best friend.

- Not at all. Takes all kinds to make the world go round, he said.

- You sit there and tell me it's all right to slander?

- No, no. I'm telling you it's all right to be homo.

- Well, she said, looking into her plate, I'm just shocked.

- Well, so am I, if it comes to that, he said, putting down his fork. I don't like your getting so intimate with him.

- Well, you're a fine one to talk, she cried, throwing down her knife. You and that Mariko person all these years. Shameless! she shouted.

The headwaiter glanced nervously at their table and then wheeled into the kitchen.

- Now, now. That was years ago, he said, smiling.

- And I think that jealousy is a very vulgar emotion, she said, referring, apparently, to his rather than to her own.

After a few more numbers from the band and some apple pie and American coffee, Mitsuko was smiling again.

- Seeing anyone else? he asked easily. Mr Paul, maybe?

- No, not at all, she lied. The only person I see at all is the Mistress.

- Now you are trying to make me jealous, he said lightly: And that is a very vulgar emotion.

She giggled, apparently pleased. Oh, you, she said.

- Why don't we go someplace, just the two of us.

- Like that place with all those American presidents staring down at us?

- You mean the Colonial? he asked, as though the idea had just struck. Well, why not?

- And get caught like last time?

- Look, that was an accident.

- Well, accidents can happen again.

- Lightning never strikes twice, he said with a little smile.

- No, but Madame Mariko might, she said, mouth a thin line.

- Please, said Hiroshi in a low voice. I need you.

- I need you too, she said candidly. But not tonight.

- When then?

- I'll think, she promised.
And when they left he swept right by the outstretched hand of Satch (Happy) Suzuki.

30

Yoranda, beautiful Eurasian, endures agony on
tatami while masked man chuckles - heu, heu, heu.
Rabo boy-hero, rushes through the night but cannot
find (forehead beaded) ratty apartment where
Sarang, secret CIA agent, has taken her. Back on
tatami Yoranda writhes and pleads. In masked man's
gloved hand an empty enema syringe. Please, someone, help me, she calls (forehead beaded). But Rabo
is attacked by rightish student thugs with chains and
staves. Pao, pao - crunch! Through blood and sweat
he sees lighted ratty tenement window. There it is!
Fists fly; thugs flee. Now, upstairs (eyes big with
resolve) and, inside, beautiful Yoranda reaches limits
of endurance (forehead beaded). New character,
bad Caucasian, sunglasses, stands gloating. Heu, heu,
heu, he gloats: You're going to get yourself dirty.
Agonized Yoranda, sphincter weakening. Turn page.

Will Rabo be in time? Will Yoranda be saved? To be continued. Read next week's *Action Comics - Japan's Best-Selling Manga Magazine*! Then: Clunk - sound of best-selling manga magazine being tossed into the waste basket. Hiroshi shook his head. Really, he said, there ought to be a law.

- What? Oh, that? asked Mariko, glancing, busy examining samples of fusuma paper. One of the girls. Midori, probably. Really she is so dumb. How about this one? Bamboo design. That's very Old Japan, don't you think?

- What could she see in it?

- There's nothing to see, said Mariko seeing that the comic book was still being discussed. It just keeps her hands busy, and her mind.

- What mind? Hiroshi wanted to know. Why, this sort of thing would give a single girl all sorts of ideas.

- Speaking of which, said Mariko, laying down the sample book: Did you get rid of her?

- I am not seeing her, lied Hiroshi with dignity.

- And did you try to stop your friend Saburo's seeing her?

- I talked with him about it, he again lied.

- And so he'll get rid of her too? she asked.

- Yes, I think so, he said, lying for the third time.

As reward, she allowed him a smile and a twinkle.

- Good, she said. So now she only has her lesbian girlfriend, the Mistress. If she has any taste for men

I dare say it will shortly be drummed out of her.

Hiroshi had an inward look, as though he was attempting to imagine this.

- You like that, don't you?

- What?

- The idea of two women together like that excites you doesn't it? Oh, you men. And sitting there relishing that perverted comic book as well.

- I was not relishing it, he said, stoutly. And I was not visualizing any embracing lesbians either. Really. I think that jealousy is a very vulgar emotion.

- I don't, said Mariko with relish. I think it natural, normal, and I don't know where women would be without it.

After this she began looking at more shoji paper samples and Midori, in a manner as unobtrusive as possible, picked up the manga and made off with it.

- Certainly doesn't improve the tone, having things like that lying around, said Hiroshi, reverting. What if a customer had found it?

- Probably already seen it, said Mariko, abstracted, holding the washi paper up to the light. Millions they sell. A week. The money. You should have got into that.

Hiroshi, now examining the washi samples and price list appended, cried: They can't mean it. Look at the prices!

- They mean it.

- But, look, this is Japanese paper. It wasn't made in Paris or something. Why so much?

- Small orders, people don't use shoji any more.

- I should have gone into the Japanese paper business, said Hiroshi, wagging his head.

Then the pep talk and the Yamato was declared open but even though it was payday few patrons appeared.

- It's the heat on the streets, said Mariko. And the new air-con here. So deliciously cool. They'll come.

- Like a deep freeze, said Hiroshi. Your girls are going to have to start wearing sweaters. Look at Midori there. She's all bumps.

- That's the price she has to pay, said Mariko mysteriously, putting the sample books away. Then, uncharacteristically, she smiled and placed a large, wet kiss on his surprised forehead. Take me home, she said in a husky whisper.

31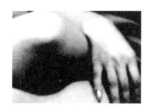

Coolidge looked down at their kiss.

Then, kiss completed, Hiroshi said: Finally.

Mitsuko at once began retouching her lips - then, noticing his irritation, said: My Sin.

- Your what?
- The shade. New. Like it? Revlon. I think.
- But why put it on now?

She looked at the rollaway table, at what was left - the major portion - of a chateaubriand for two, some nameless vegetable, an empty bottle of corked claret.

- We've finished, she answered.
- We haven't even begun, he said as smoothly as though practiced and ran a hand over her shoulder.
- I am not about to be apprehended again, she said.
- You won't be, he said stooping to kiss that shoulder.
- What makes you so certain? Her spies are everywhere.
- I paid him a fortune.
- Oh, you did? That was smart.
- We will not be disturbed, he said and smiled in a knowing manner.
- It would make no difference if we were, said Mitsuko putting My Sin back in her purse. Because you must reaiize, Watanabe-san, that a girl can't go around being compromised. I came here only to talk.

- To the Colonial, to talk? he asked, incredulous, exasperated.

- Yes. it isn't as though we were not old friends and couldn't come where we want for a quiet chat now, is it? And I wanted to talk about my future. You realize I may have to get married.

- What, what, what? We haven't even done any thing yet.

She regarded him as though from a height, then added: I was referring to the fact that if I fail in my ambition to open my own small and exclusive place, I may be forced, as so many girls are, to marry as an economic measure. To have enough to eat, she added lest he fail to comprehend.

Hiroshi seemed to comprehend: Well, why don't you go to your friend, Saburo? he asked.

- Tanaka-san and I are just friends.

- Well, that's apparently all we are too, you and me.

- I am so sorry, Watanabe-san, said Mitsuko look-ing gently at him: I had thought we were perhaps something more. I see I have made an error.

- Wa! cried Hiroshi, irritated, exasperated. Then he grabbed her and began covering her face with kisses. She struggled and the rollaway table rolled away. While grappling with the girl Hiroshi looked around for the button, perhaps intending to throw her onto the couch once it was located.

- Help, cried Mitsuko softly as Hiroshi, still clutching her, stabbed at where he thought the console was. The table bumped against the wall and Coolidge trembled.

- You've got to understand, said Hiroshi, explaining as they struggled. A man can stand only so much. Ah!

He had found the button, pushed, jumped nimbly to one side to spare his ankles, pushing the girl skillfully at the same time so that she would land, confused, defenceless, on the provident bed. In fact, however, since the sofa failed to appear at all she landed in a heap on the floor.

- Brute! she cried in outrage.

- Oh! It must be broken, he said, then pushed a few more futile times. Look, I am sorry. That was an accident.

- And I thought you were a gentleman! she said, sitting up.

- This is fraudulent, he said, seriously: Imagine the Colonial without its foldout sofas. I could have them in court for this.

- I could have you in court! she cried: You deliberately threw me to the floor.

- Now, now, he said, bending to pick her up. She slapped at him and struggled to her feet, then sat on the chair and cowered.

- Look, I'm sorry. He tried a little smile.

- You keep away from me. Oh, you really had me fooled, Watanabe-san. I had thought you were a gentleman, a nice, older person who was interested in my career, and what do I find? This! She indicated the chateaubriand, Coolidge, Hiroshi himself.

He knelt on the floor in front of her: I was out of my mind, I was mad at the very thought of you and Saburo.

- Nothing much to think about there. And what about you and that older woman?

- It's not the same thing at all, and, Mitsuko-san, jealousy is a very vulgar emotion.

- You should talk!

But he cajoled and, finally, she allowed herself a pretty pout, then laughed at all the lipstick on his face, and he was careful to be rueful and comic.

After that he listened in apparent concentration while she told him all about the kind of intimate little place of her own that she would like to open up. Perhaps it resembled a similar scene with Madame Mariko years before. In any event, Hiroshi appeared weary, though he kept blinking his eyes to make them bright and interested.

- Well, we'll think about it. We can't promise anything, you know. I'm not in the bar business, am I? And the new Yamato is going to cost a pretty penny, let me tell you.

Having told her this, he attempted another kiss

and was gently repulsed, the singular reason being that she did not want to get My Sin all over him.

32

Threw her to the floor, forced himself upon her, his body heavy against hers. With what small strength remained, the poor girl had cried for help but of course in that den such calls were an hourly if unanswered occurrence. No one came. She had had to defend herself. Fortunately, she escaped with her virtue intact

This was the burden of the telephone call Saburo had received at the Lovely Boy just before Mariko, a sixth sense perhaps informing, had stormed in, to the consternation of the customary clientele, and demanded to know if Hiroshi had really stopped seeing Mitsuko as promised - or what?

- Look. You're upsetting the customers, said Saburo, looking around at the white faces, the injured glances, - any woman was bad enough, but a furious one was worse. Indeed, the very social fabric seemed threatened.

- Well, I'm sorry, I'm sure, but this is important. One just can't help worrying about him.

Since this was a sentiment - worrying about him - shared by the other customers, accord was quickly restored with many an understanding nod.

- Well, I can't say that I know much, said Saburo evasively.

- But you can't say that you don't. I thought as much. You men are so transparent.

Those about her nodded in emphatic agreement and Mariko went on: And it isn't as though I hadn't asked you to find out. You're my friend, after all.

- I've not seen him recently, you know.

- Well, then, you could have asked her. You've seen her often enough, haven't you?

The customers now plainly felt for the misused woman and a few of them glared at the master of the Lovely Boy.

- Now, look here, Mariko-san.

- Just give her a straight answer, poor thing, said a young man with earrings and a slave-bracelet.

- Well, I don't - began Saburo.

- Trying to keep him for yourself, eh? asked a youth in a sports sweater and mascara. I think that this is just plain low, taking another person's man, ugh!

Such was the condemnation (general after a while) that Saburo allowed that Hiroshi had perhaps seen Mitsuko a time or two. And such was Mariko's skill and determination that after a bit she (and the others in the Lovely Boy) had discovered both the place and the time.

- But I'm sure nothing occurred, said Saburo, sweating.

This was hooted down by the sophisticated clientele and Mariko told them that earlier she had actually caught the culprit in the act. This was much exclaimed at.

- And now he's back with the same slut, probably in the very same hotel and he tells me that nothing's occurred.

The crowd carried on and Saburo, perhaps feeling he had to prove that nothing had indeed occurred, was soon explaining the whole thing as he had heard it.

When they were informed of the attempted rape there was a division of opinion among the customers. Some were indignant but others assumed faraway expressions that might have indicated discretion or might have betokened longing. Mariko laughed out loud at this but soon saw that it was more to her advantage to appear furious.

- So that is how he keeps his promises! All those reassurances! False! Every one! And him your classmate too! Oh, I am so angry!

- And so she ought be, eh fellows? said one of

the older patrons: We've all had experiences like that, right? Oh, men and their false ways!

Over the cries of assent Saburo shouted to make himself heard; Just don't tell him that I told you.

- Of course not, said Mariko who, having gotten what she wanted, was now preparing to go, shaking hands all around, and saying farewell to her sympathetic new friends.

33

- And to have to hear it from your best friend, your classmate, she screamed. Emiko fled into the *dames* and Hiroshi, still dazed, cried: What?

Mariko had attacked at once, shouting, crying, clawing the air, accurately accusing him of all that he had done, or at least attempted.

- Yes, your best friend, she said, lowering her voice to sarcastic depths. Of course, I am fortunate in that he is the better friend to me, that he could not see me going on in trusting ignorance, that he took pity on me. He told me *all*!

This went on for some time until Hiroshi, growing brave, or at least exasperated, said: But, I didn't do anything.

- Well, it was not for want of trying.

- It was all an unfortunate accident.

- Most unfortunate - most unfortunate too that I knew all about the other times.

- What other times? There was only one, the time before.

- Yes, the time I saw, with my own eyes. And this one now I must hear. With - my - own - ears.

- It would be difficult to hear of it in any other way, said Hiroshi, attempting levity.

- And this person calls himself a man, she said, disregarding, as though to a third party: He goes around attacking helpless women.

- She was scarcely that, he complained.

- Beast! I wasn't talking about the little viper. I meant me. Helpless, unable to defend herself against your lying and your cheating. Oh! And she began throwing pillows about.

After that she settled down and things were calmer.

Pillows back in place, she sat in the repaired but still fake Empire chair, he on the real pouffe.

- You realize, of course, things can never be quite the same between us.

- Oh, come now, Mariko.

- The plate of friendship may be mended but the

crack always shows, she said, perhaps quoting.

- Oh, really now.

- No, she said, holding up her hand as though to fend off further insult. It is quite simple. I-can-no-longer-trust-you. You gave your word. You broke it. It is that simple. No, please, Watanabe-san. No more explanations. You forget how soft, how tender, how easily wounded are a woman's emotions . . .

- Soft? Tender? And five minutes ago the help was scattering in terror.

At this she gave a weary little smile: Of course, we can still have a relationship, you and I. After all, a matter of years is not over in a matter of minutes. But it will have to be of a different nature. More businesslike.

She interrupted herself to ask sharply: What are you doing?

For Hiroshi, as though disconsolate, was wandering about the room, looking under the pillows, under the tables.

- Oh, nothing, he said. Just something I was reading.

- Reading? Oh, you want the new issue of *Action Comics*, I imagine, she said. Well, Midori hasn't brought it in yet. You might try the toilet.

- Emiko's still cowering there.

- You men! You just wanted to find out what happened to Yoranda, beautiful Eurasian, she began, then stopped as though realizing that in attempting to incriminate him she was incriminating herself.

Of this, however, he did not take advantage and she, perhaps emboldened, returned to financial matters. For the next hour, until the first customers appeared, she talked about how she was going to have real period screens and electrified but otherwise authentic andon lanterns, and that all the girls would have to appear in quite high-class kimono.

34

- You said eleven o'clock and I've been sitting in this creepy place for over half an hour, complained Mitsuko.

- Well, very sorry I'm sure, said Sumire who was showing a tendency toward independence. But tonight was the ninety-second installment of 'A Mother's Heart' and I just had to see it. Her daughter's pregnant, her son's in jail, and she's got cancer. I cried! Then: Besides, this place is no more creepy than the one you work in.

She gazed around the Gambling Girl, females in

jeans lounging with beer and staring at the two pretty interlopers in their designer dresses.

- No, she amended, I guess yours is less creepy. I hope they don't try to pick us up.

- They just might, said Mitsuko. Why else would we be here all mousey over our Coca-Colas?

- Well, it was your idea we meet here. It could have been My Pussy.

- My Pussy's just as creepy nowadays, said Mitsuko.

After a time, however, they forgot their admirers and over Tina Turner shouted back and forth at each other.

- I am definitely over him, shouted Mitsuko.

- Which one? her friend wanted to know.

- Watanabe. The older one. He's no gentleman. Though I will continue to see him. I have my future to think of.

- What about the other one?

- Oh, Tanaka-san. He's so dreamy. And handsome. And he's got this little-boy grin that just kills you. Not that he's so young, you understand. Actually, he's kind of - well, craggy.

Sumire looked into her Coke. She seemed to be thinking. Then: He's up for grabs.

- Hiroshi-san? No. I told you I had my plans.

- Well, you can't have both, said Sumire suddenly, setting her jaw.

- Well, I would like to know just why not, said her friend, showing her teeth. They are my friends, after all.

- It's not fair, said Sumire, stubborn.

- Fair? Look, Ogawa, you just go out and make your own friends. I need them both, one for business and one for romance. And it is going to work out. I've got this gut reaction, she said, using a fashionable phrase.

- You've simply got to learn to doubt your gut reaction, said Sumire, suddenly bossy.

- You just mess out now. Go find your own friends.

- I can't, I'm not pretty, pouted Sumire, shutting her little eyes.

- You are pretty enough for all normal purposes, shouted Mitsuko, exasperated, and several of the listening women at the bar applauded.

- You keep your voice down, said Sumire and would have said more had not the waitress, safety pin in ear, put before them two large draft beers. Compliments of them over there, she said, before striding away.

Both looked at the bar where all five of the large jeaned women were holding mugs aloft, grinning. Drink up, called one: More where that came from.

- Oh, God, said Sumire who sometimes affected Christianity.

- Follow me, called Mitsuko and the two were shortly away, out under the motorcycled young lady in neon, into the dark late-summer heat.

35

Tokyo twinkled and Mitsuko played with her pie, then looked up and said: September already. A pause, then: Well, I just don't know how she knew. Every last detail.

- She's got her spies just everywhere, said Saburo uneasily.

- But Watanabe-san said he paid them off. Of course, there may have been more. Anyway, he says it was awful.

- From what you told me on the phone must have been pretty awful for you too, said Saburo warmly.

- Yes, she said, simply. It was. But this is worse. Now, he tells me, she is definitely going to see my employer And if she does that and tells what happened, well, I am out of a job. I'll have to get married. Economic measure.

- No need to do anything that drastic, said Saburo running a hand along the back of her chair. Something will turn up.

- I wish I had your hope, she said, as though sincere. You always seem to see the bright side of things. Me, I just can't seem to.

His arm now around her shoulders, he moved closer, his mouth at her ear: Something will turn up, you'll see.

She turned, as though just now noticing the encircling grasp: Tanaka-san, are you married?

- Well, no, I'm not.

- At your age. She sounded shocked.

- Never found the right person, he said, eyes downcast but little smile forming.

- That's no excuse, she said. But then in any event, you aren't lonely. You have Madame Mariko, I believe.

- Nothing of the sort, he said virtuously.

- Watanabe-san believes that you do.

- Hiroshi is sometimes just plain funny. First he tries to rape you and then he goes on and tells lies about me. But he was always strange, even as a schoolboy.

- Well, at least I believe that you, Tanaka-san, would never attempt to rape a young lady.

- Never, said Saburo, firmly, Then, with that smile of his: Not that a little old-fashioned seduction would be beneath me. If I thought I had a chance, that is.

- Man makes his opportunities, she said, certainly quoting.

At once the arm was tighter around her shoulder. This time she ignored it.

- A girl needs a friend, she said: Someone in whom she can confide.

- Of course she does, said Saburo, moving closer.

- Me - she laughed, as though at herself - I've only really got one friend. And she's a girl. Her name is Sumire. We are very close.

She turned to see what effect this information might have. If Watanabe-san was excited at the thought of two women together, as he had once all but admitted that he was, perhaps Tanaka-san was too. This perhaps was why she repeated: Very.

- Envy you that, you women. Close relationships. Men don't have them much. Not, at any rate, as a general rule.

It was not to Mitsuko's purpose to mention the Lovely Boy and the close relationships to be found there so she did not. Rather: Yes, she said, a good neck to cry on.

- We men rarely have such, he said as though sincerely sorry for this.

- But I sometimes think it unhealthy. Sumire and I are that close, she lied. One wants a man to come and take one away from all this.

Here she looked him full in the face, but he, sipping his coffee, merely observed that, yes, he could see how one would.

And such was his wide experience that no matter how Mitsuko tried, she could not get him to commit himself to anything further than a desire for a dinner at the Colonial.

- After all, I see a lot of you, he said, and everyone gets to compromise you but me. He began ticking them off on his fingers: the Mistress, Sumire-san, Hiroshi.

- Oh, no, don't! she cried and the headwaiter dropped a tureen.

Saburo turned to look and then said: In fact, a person could say that you lead a person on. Not that I would, of course, say that, that is. Live and let live. That's what I say.

While the soup was being mopped up, the waiters wheeling about in the gloom, he rested his benevolent but slightly impatient gaze upon her. Then suddenly, galvanized, sat up. What's that? he asked, as though in trepidation.

She opened her eyes wide but by this time he was smiling at his surprise. It was just that Satch (Happy) Suzuki and the Streamliners were playing a new tune: 'Sentimental Journey.'

36

- We can talk here, said Hiroshi.

- What? yelled Mr. Paul.

- Talk, Hiroshi shouted in return.

The Honolulu Cabaret - girls squealed, men bellowed, speakers blared and one small girl popped up and said: Hi, my name is Momoko.

- No, no, shouted Hiroshi, fighting her off as they were pulled through the portal, past pasteboard palm trees, real coconuts, and pushed into their seats. One girl sat on either side of each and one each on their laps. These at once began to order.

- Later, later, shouted Hiroshi. My friend and I want to talk.

- Talk! shouted the girls above the din and looked at each other with round, mystified eyes.

Left more or less alone, the two zipped themselves up and then Paul shouted: If you wanted to talk why did you take me to a place like this?

- Because, Hiroshi shouted back, if Mariko has the place bugged she won't be able to hear us above the din. No, don't laugh. Reilly, I think she's a witch. She knows things she has no way of knowing. Had a little falling-out with Mitsuko-san the other day, and no sooner did I get back than she knew all, and I mean all about it. It was uncanny. I think I'm going mad.

Mr. Paul nodded, as though in agreement, then shouted: Mitsuko wanted to know. Did you like her.

- Oh, she did?
- Yes. Liked her enough to get her her own place.
- No, no, no. I just can't afford that.
- I won't be here much longer. In Tokyo. I'll tell her. Before I go.
- No, no. Don't do that, Hiroshi yelled, perhaps believing that then the attractive young lady would have no further use for him. No, he said, just tell her that she ought to make some kind of investment.
- Some kind of what? shouted Paul.
- Oh, this awful noise! No, what I mean is she's nice to me, I'm nice to her. One hand washes the other.
- You want her to wash her hands?
- No, no, no. It's an idiom. She scratches my back, I scratch hers.
- You want to scratch her back?

Further conversation was prevented by Momoko and her friends breaking through their defenses. Soon the place was alive with girls and orders were flying.

- Oh! Ugh! What is this? shouted Mr. Paul.

- She's demonstrating her talent, guessed Hiroshi.

- Her what? The reply was lost in the squeals of the girls - beer, squid, Kraft on Ritz having arrived.

- Ouch, that hurt! said Mr. Paul. Stop it!

Momoko laughed and scurried under the table.

- No, no no. Stop it! cried Hiroshi feeling the nimble fingers. He kicked at random and was rewarded with loud cries. Then he looked at Paul and shrugged: After all they have to make a living too. Anyway, you tell her what I said.

Mr. Paul perhaps did not hear. Oh, no, he shouted: She's putting squid on me!

37

- Nice tune that, said Mariko and began accompanying. 'Want to take a sentimental journey,' she sang. Satch (Happy) Suzuki looked over and smiled paternally. Reminds you of the old times, doesn't it, Hiroshi-san, she said.

- Forty years ago, he said.

- Of course, I was just a babe then, she declared,

looking at Tokyo twinkling below. And whoever would have thought . . . she said, perhaps referring to the far-flung city, perhaps not.

- I too was a child, he said.

- Of course you were, she agreed as though commiserating.

- I wanted to be a policeman, he said, listening to the tune.

- And I wanted to be a nurse, she said, smiling fondly as though at an earlier, forgotten self. And remember the sweet potatoes?

- Nothing but sweet potatoes, and that American rice.

- We were so poor, she marveled, and just look at us now.

- I remember when a chicken was a fortune, he said softly, looking at his plate.

- And my mother used to paint her stockings on. Strong tea. And the back seam was indelible pencil.

- And just look at us now, he marveled.

- Well, we worked hard, she recalled.

- Put up with a lot, he remembered.

- Did our best, she stated, and 'Sentimental Journey' came to its sticky close.

- Well, said Madame Mariko blinking, as though just awakened: I've been thinking. Perhaps I have been too harsh on certain parties.

Hiroshi seemed instantly suspicious.

- Yes, Mitsuko Koyama. Perhaps I have been bit hard on her. So, I think perhaps I will make it up, invite her to the Yamato for old times' sake. And I heard that she is with this nice new girlfriend of hers, so I might ask them both.

- Going to ask the Mistress as well? he inquired, sarcasm implicit.

- No, probably not, she said, as though she had considered this. She's doubtless jealous enough of dear Mitsuko's new little friend as it is. No sense in creating a scene.

- Are you going to create one yourself, once you get them there?

- Really! For what do you take me? No, I am a woman of some experience and would find it quite beneath my dignity to appear to argue with some-one so fresh, so green, so untried.

- Mariko, what are you up to?

- Me? She splayed her hand against her breast.

And he could get nothing further from her except that she expected him to make the invitations and then make himself scarce. It was to be a little party for just the three of them.

- Just us girls together, she said.

And, in answer to further questions: September already. Not that it's not as hot as ever. You'll remember now and ask them for next week because the week after we are closing the place for the remodeling. Any day except Friday. That's payday and the place will be packed. Oh, is that the moon? Yes, it is. The autumn moon! Oh, Hiroshi, would you be a dear and go give something to that nice man smiling away there and ask him to play our song again?

38

- Yes, it does seem that autumn is on its way, said Mariko with a smile, little finger extended. I thought this morning I detected the slightest nip in the air.

- Indeed, said Mitsuko, respectifully.

- She has such beautiful things, politely observed Sumire, looking down at the tea set, the Sevres one, the one usually locked up in the glass-fronted Louis Seize for all to see but not to touch.

- She certainly does, said Mitsuko, equally polite, little finger equally extended.

- Yes, Mitsuko dear would remember, wouldn't she? You see we were colleagues once. For all too short a time I am sorry to say. Do try one of these.

She pushed forward the plate of small cakes, brought perhaps at the nearest Cozy Corner. *Petits fours*, she added.

- Yum, said Sumire, helping herself to a *tarte mirabelle*.

- It all seems so long ago, said Mitsuko looking at the golf trophies, the chandelier, the fish.

- Yes, a lot of water has gone over the dam, said her hostess, using the popular idiom. Then, suddenly: Look your last.

Mitsuko, startled, put up her hands, as though to defend herself against pistol or dagger.

- All of this is going to be changed, Mariko continued, unnoticing: French is out. Japanese is in. The old Yamato is going to live up to its name. We are going Old Japan. Tatami, shoji, fusuma, the works.

There was much exclaiming at this and soon the three of them were deep into interior decoration talk. After a time, Mariko, apparently deciding time had come to come to the point, said: It is so good of you to come. Friends are so precious.

Mitsuko, reading dismissal, picked up her purse.

- No, no, my dear. Of what are you thinking? You've only just come. Another cake? More tea? No? Well, I was just thinking how really good good friends are, how necessary.

The girls waited.

- Take now a good friend who I believe you two must also know, at least he's mentioned you. Such a good friend. So necessary to one. I refer to Tanaka-san, our own Saburo-sama.

- Hello there, called a masculine voice and down the stairs, through the foyer, and into the Yamato came Hiroshi.

- Oh, there you are. Having a little tea party?

Mariko looked up, angry: I thought you weren't coming.

- Found some free time, said Hiroshi, unabashed.

Mariko carefully put down her *gateau aux cassis*. I am very surprised. There are no extra cups.

- Oh, don't bother about me, he said rocking back and forth, regarding the sitting women with apparent pleasure. Then: There is one of your number whom I have not yet had the pleasure of being presented to.

Sumire Ogawa was introduced. He bowed and she, perhaps out of deference to the European surroundings, extended her hand.

After that there was the silence of Mariko's evident displeasure, one which Hiroshi attempted to break with small questions as to how they liked the cakes.

Finally, apparently coming to a resolve, Mariko turned to her female guests and said: I mentioned earlier that the Yamato will shorty be remodeled.

Well, at the end of next month, just before the official opening, we are going to have a small preview party which will also serve as farewell to a dear friend, a foreigner, however one whom I believe that you, Mitsuko dear, have already had the pleasure of meeting. And it is to this small affair that I wish to extend an invitation to you both. All dear friends, all together for the last time.

After the guests had gone and Midori had collected the sticky plates and listened to her employer's shrill admonitions to be careful with that tea set, Mariko turned to Hiroshi with a hiss. You were not to be here, she said.

- I know, but -

- You promised. And you came in at just the wrong time. You saw what happened. In effect you destroyed my little tea party.

-You did not get to say what you wanted to, said Hiroshi, sage.

- That's right, said Mariko, honest for a change.

- You wanted to warn them off Saburo.

- Them? Is the mousey one on to him too?

- How would I know? I'm not the one traveling in that crowd. I never see any of them anymore.

- Well, he mentioned this Sumire person but I don't think he's actually met her yet. No, I wanted to somehow get it through that Mitsuko's thick little head that she should leave Saburo alone.

Hiroshi was surprised at such apparent frankness. So, it all comes out, he said: You are that interested in my classmate.

Mariko sighed, apparently at further thick headedness: No, no. Silly. it was for your sake.

He started.

- Mind that cake plate. Yes, your sake. It wouldn't be fair, you see, I told myself, if Hiroshi-san could not have his Mitsuko then Saburo-san shouldn't either.

At which Hiroshi simply sat down.

39

- It was his coming in that did it, said Mitsuko. She couldn't spin her web in front of him, you see.

- So that was Hiroshi-san, said Sumire with half a smile.

- Look, I never said he was handsome or anything.

- But you didn't mention the tummy, the hairline.

- What do you expect at his age? Matchi-kun? she asked, naming a current teenage favorite. And besides, one does not go out with him for romance, for goodness sake. Then, as though thinking: And they're classmates too. So different. You'd never know.

- Compared to Saburo-san? But Japanese men classmates always act like married couples, was Sumire's sudden sage observation

- But that's male bonding. That's different, said Mitsuko, knowledgeable.

- Well, anyway, said Sumire, as though in answer, I see what you mean about Madame Mariko. Scared me.

- And she was being *nice* to you.

- Excuse me, said the waiter, now a travesty of himself: I've got to mop up that sick over in the corner.

- Oh, dear. I didn't see it. Let's move. And they moved to a further table and then, when they found a large young man under it, to one yet further.

- Yes, My Pussy's certainly lost its tone, affirmed Sumire. Then: Of course, she didn't want to invite us at all. It was simply that she couldn't carry through her plot. And so she will have to do it at the party itself. How exciting.

- She must be wildly, madly in love with him, poor man.

- Saburo-san, said Sumire, intuiting, small eyes squinting.

- Right, Saburo-san. She is so jealous of me that it

shows in her eyes. Did you see those crazy glints?

- I think jealousy is a very vulgar emotion, said Sumire.

- I think she is a very vulgar person, said Mitsuko.

Several men in trench coats came in and began to examine the body.

- But we're going, aren't we?

- We?

- Surely, said Sumire. I was invited as well. You heard that.

- I suppose so, said Mitsuko ungraciously, then: I have an idea. I know how to make Madame Mariko just sick. Why don't you play up to Saburo-san when you meet him. You know, bat your eyes, things like that.

- Oh, said Sumire, I don't know anything about things like that.

- Well, pretend you do then, said Mitsuko unfeelingly. It won't get you anywhere, of course, but it will make her feel just awful.

- Well, if you say so.

- Maybe we should meet him beforehand, said Mitsuko, thinking. That way it would be easier to make her jealous. And less sudden for him, too.

- Well, you just tell me what to do, said Sumire seemingly helpless.

- Excuse me, said the waiter scratching his cropped, bruised head. But might I ask you to pay

168

up and leave? We're being raided, you see, I think. He looked at the detectives in their trench coats.

- They let it get out of hand, said Mitsuko to Sumire as they left. This happens when you let something get out of hand. It will be closed now. Poor My Pussy.

- I didn't want to come anymore anyway, said Sumire with a show of spirit. It was sort of getting to be the dregs. Let's only go to decent places from now on.

40

Shortly before midnight the taxi stopped and out piled the two girls and the man.

- Should be somewhere around here, said Mitsuko peering. Never been here but it was recommended as a fun place and since *we're* taking *you* out tonight I thought nothing but the best.

- Nothing but the best, echoed Sumire, vivaciously.

They paused before a small door covered with plastic ivy, over it a lighted purple sign containing a single kanji.

- Can't read it, said Saburo as the two stared at it over his shoulder. Sumire began tracing the kanji pattern in her palm, shaking her head the while.

- The place is supposed to be called Kon, said Mitsuko. Is that Kon?

- I wouldn't know. But *con* means vagina in French.

- Oh, well, then, this is it, said Mitsuko and pushed open the door, to reveal a large, dark, square room, brick-patterned wallpaper, black-painted chairs and tables, checkered tablecloths, candles in bottles, and lots more plastic ivy. The middle of the room was cleared, as though for dancing.

There was no dancing. A fat young man was hanging from a rude scaffold and two girls in boots were burning with cigarette lighters the hair from his armpits. Another man was bent over a chair, reddened buttocks exposed, and yet another was bound on the floor, a woman sitting on his face.

Rising, whip in hand, the latter approached. A table for three, please, said Mitsuko. A table near the show.

The woman showed no sign of having heard, looked at the party, then extended an imperious arm, her whip pointing directly to the door through which they had entered.

- Suzuki-san sent us, said Saburo, suddenly. We're friends of his.

- Well, you ought have said so at once. One can't be too careful. Can't have just anyone walking in off the street.

After which she led them to a table.

- Who is Suzuki-san? wondered Mitsuko.

- There is always, everywhere, a Suzuki-san, you see, said Saburo with that smile of his: And everyone knows him.

The standing woman with the whip suddenly turned to him: I have been waiting for you, she said ominously.

He looked suitably startled, sat down.

- I have some pretty things for you to do, she continued, drawing closer. Thought about it a lot, eh? Lay there in bed at night and abused yourself, thinking about someone like me, eh? Polluted yourself, dirtied yourself, while you thought of someone like me standing over you and making you do unspeakable things, eh? This was recited rather than spoken. Then she advanced, groin in his face.

Mitsuko looked at Saburo, back against the wall, and then said. No, no. Suzuki-san thought we'd be interested in general, not in particular. We just came to observe.

- Oh. Well, it would have been better if someone had said so at first, said the woman, adding: I am Madame Kon. Then they all shook hands and a boy appeared with glasses, ice and a full bottle of Chivas Regal.

- Chin-chin, said Madame Kon raising her glass.

- Nice place you have here, said Saburo, looking about with interest. The plump, singed young man had now been pushed over a hassock and was exposing a large, white rump. One of the girls in boots was languidly beating it with a single slipper.

Sumire, little eyes now enormous, turned to her friend and whispered: Which one is the sadist?

- Oh, she is, said Madame Kon pleasantly. The other one is called a masochist. Actually he's with one of the better trading companies.

- All the girls here are sadists, you see, she continued with a motherly smile. And the men are, with the possible exception of your friend here, consequently masochists.

Saburo smiled, nodded, indicating perhaps that life was interesting, varied, that it took all kinds to make the world go round. Then he said: Nice show.

This was an error. Madame Kon drew herself up, eyes flashing: This is no show. We do not encourage those who come merely to look. This is authentic. Love, passion, pain. We do not allow *tourists*!

She spat out the word and then, softening slightly, explained: You see, we think of ourselves as a family. A family coming together of an evening to pursue its mutual interests. We do not encourage outsiders.

Saburo, apparently not used to being spoken to in this manner, drew himself up and said: Anyone can walk in.

Madame Kon smiled mysteriously. But, they do not. Only the truly interested enter.

This was true. People did not just walk in to places. But the police can just walk in, he said.

- And so they do, said Madame Kon, arranging the black lace at her thighs: All the time. They walk in to discover if any of the girls are naked. And none of us ever are. And so they walk out.

- Saburo stared at the large, bare rump, now quite red, and then surveyed the room A gentleman in partial undress was on the floor, barking. Several others were sitting and leafing through large photo albums.

- They are awaiting their turns, said Madame Kon, smiling: Their precious moments in Paradise.

Sumire, looking more and more like a mouse, made a small convulsive movement.

- Don't you be frightened, said Saburo kindly: They don't discipline girls here.

One of the booted girls went among the guests, kicking a shin here, slapping a face there, then bent over a man and opened his trousers with one quick hand. This was followed by a ripping sound and a flicker of concern on the man's face. The girl had torn off a wide band of adhesive, taking with it, apparently, much else.

- That was applied just two hours ago by the clock, said Madame Kon, noting Saburo's interest: We work on a schedule here, quite efficient, actually.

- For example, she continued, pointing to the floor. A pair of feet, until then unnoticed, protruded from under the red-checkered tablecloth. Raising it, she displayed naked buttocks bound with rope, like a roast with string.

- He has been there an hour now, she said, and he's almost done. She might have been speaking of something in the oven.

Saburo leaned forward, regarding the bound patron with interest and, it would seem, approval. Kind of a production line method, eh? Good, sound system. And makes for an efficient turnover as well.

There was a low whine from under the table. Madame Kon bent over to investigate and was heard to say: Oh, the rope hurts does it? Well, I'll really give you something to complain about. Aki, bring me the shoehorn. Then: Oh, that girl, I'll go get it myself.

- Interesting place, said Sumire, having dropped her rodent ways as soon as Saburo looked at her. She now blew smoke from her nostrils and gazed at him in what she must have thought a veiled manner.

Saburo looked at her with new interest and Mitsuko regarded her with puzzled alarm.

- Hi, I'm Aki, said one of the booted girls, suddenly standing in front of them. And I have been sent to make you happy during Madame's absence, and I have some pretty things for you to do.

She began by addressing herself to Saburo. Thought about it a lot, eh? Lay in bed at night and abused yourself -

- No, no, said Mitsuko. We're friends of Suzuki-san.

- Which Suzuki-san? Aki wanted to know: There are dozens of them here. They're all Suzukis.

- Well, he's a friend of Madame Kon's.

- They're all Madame Kon's friends. Who are you folks anyway? And she put a booted foot on the table.

So Saburo said, perhaps thinking to make things better: You see we're here to study. Sort of apprentice sadists.

It did not make things better: Then what are you doing here? she demanded. Look, you either got to be a masochist or a friend. You can't just come in here like this. Hey, Madame Kon!

But Madame Kon was otherwise occupied. She had a middle-aged gentleman by the ear and was determinedly pulling him towards the gents.

- Excuse me, said Saburo. Could you please ask the person under the table to stop it? He's ruining my shine.

Aki lifted the tablecloth and brought her palm down hard on the trussed rump. You just settle down there, she called. And don't lick the shoes.

She shook her head. Such pigs, she said. Get carried away, lick just anything. And the carpet such a mess afterwards.

- I thought it was the candlewax, said Saburo, looking about him.

- It's not, said Aki. Then, upon hearing faint cries coming from the toilet. Oh, that's where she went.

- Are you really pathological perverts? Saburo asked politely.

- We could not do a proper job if we were not so inclined, said Aki civilly. But I must say, the work isn't easy.

She sat down as though to take a weight off her boots, then explained: Take this one here now. Company president. Polyester, I think. Every other night. Comes in when we open and sometimes not even finished when we close. Takes hours, and all that time down there in the dark and we got to remember and look him up now and again or else he complains. A big bother. Oh, shit.

A gentleman in a dog collar bowed and knelt before her.

- No more horsy, she said. He neighed enthusiastically and so she sighed, climbed on, rode off.

- So this is the new fun place. Well, it makes me

see that I have things easy at Elle, said Mitsuko.

- I hope they get paid lots, like hardship pay, said Sumire.

- We'll find out when we get the bill, said Mitsuko.

- Maybe that's why only company presidents can afford to come, was the opinion of her friend.

- Well, said Saburo with his little smile, I must say you girls know how to take a gent to some pretty novel places.

- Are you enjoying it?

- Well, yes. From an economic point of view she's got a fantastic setup.

- That's what we're afraid of, said Mitsuko: It will cost so much and we wanted to take you out. You have done so much for me.

- Well, little bit more wouldn't hurt, said Saburo all but patting his wallet.

Madame Aki, returned, was explaining something to the other booted girl. Then she turned to a man standing there in his boxer shorts and introduced the two. They bowed. He began a gesture, perhaps habitual, but had, of course, no pockets in which to carry his business-card.

- And, be careful, she said to the girl. He's just got out of the hospital. Traction. We don't want to hurt him.

Then, aware that this last had been overheard,

and that the underweared gentleman was looking puzzled and unhappy, she turned and slapped him across the face. Reassured, he beamed and trotted off after his tormentor.

- There, said Madame Kon, sitting again with them: Enjoying ourselves?

- I've been admiring your setup, said Saburo.

- Yes, I feel we do our bit, she said, smiling. Trying to make the world a happier place, relieving tensions you might say. Either of you girls care for a job? I always have room here for new, young talent.

- No, thank you, said both girls at the same time.

And they talked on, mainly about the financial possibilities of such a specialized venture as this, until Mitsuko asked for the ladies and Madame Kon went to show her and keep the customers from throwing themselves under her feet on the way and then Sumire turned, veiled her eyes and said: I must have you.

- I beg your pardon, said Saburo.

- We were made for each other, she perhaps quoted. Then: Take me to the Colonial. Have your way with me.

- I think maybe this place is getting to you. Perhaps I'd better take you two girls home.

- Take *her* home. Take *me* with you. And Sumire batted her eyelashes and put her hand on his knee, quickly removing it when Mitsuko returned.

- Really, she said, sitting down: That toilet!

- We consider it an extension of our rumpus room here. explained Madame Kon.

- And on the way this man came out from under the chair and licked my leg. Ugh!

- Well, they are good boys at heart, you know. Just having a bit of fun, was Madame Kon's belief. It takes all kinds to make this little old world go round.

And amid such generalities Mitsuko did not apparently notice that there had been a particular difference during her absence and that an understanding now informed the relations of her two friends.

Aki waved, Madame Kon bowed, Saburo put a considerably thinner wallet back into his pocket and Mitsuko did not even guess.

41

- I thought you'd be here, said Mariko settling on a stool. The young men on either side moved rapidly away. She looked at the sporting prints and said: Well, it's a bit more manly than the Lovely Boy.

- For the time being, said Saburo settling beside her. Going to be bulldozed.

- Forever why? It seems decent enough to me, she said looking at the prim young men sitting about.

- High price of land here in Shinjuku, said Saburo. The whole block's going. Then they're putting up a high-rise,

- Full of homo bars, I suppose. Like a boutique collection.

- No, rent's too high for homo bars anymore. They'll have to find someplace else to go.

She looked around. Poor things, she said audibly: Homeless

- Just as well, said Saburo, informing: The Regency here is for the boys to meet foreign men and now, just like my place, they have this No Foreigners Allowed sign on the door.

- Doesn't that defeat the purpose?

- You got to be safe, you know. This AIDS thing is going to end up costing us a lot. Business has fallen off.

- Well, I should think so. A financial calamity. Then: Still think it's Japan's greatest growth indus-try?

- Nipped in the bud it would seem, was the rueful reply. Then: Shame, too. Just when it was getting respectable.

He shook his head: Too bad - first the disease and now the high price of land. Of course, Lovely Boy is a little different. It's still hygienically and financially feasible. We didn't allow foreigners in from the first so no one misses them. It's just for our own kind, you know. And since the location's not all that choice the rent's not impossible yet. Not like here.

Mariko looked around at the tartan, the prints, the oxford collars, the knit ties, the argyle socks, the hush puppies. Trad, she said: Trad and classic, she added, maybe quoting. Its all coming back now - tradition.

- Country's going to the right, agreed Saburo.

- No, I meant the new old Yamato. We're redecorating. I've got to do something. Never seen the Ginza so bad. Perhaps the bubble has truly burst, she said, truly quoting. Then, following a logic of her own: You seen Hiroshi?

- Is that why you tracked me down here?

- Tracked you down! Fine choice of language. No, not at all. I simply called the Lovely Boy and they said you were here.

- Yes, little business talk. And he winked at the bartender. But, no - not at all, he said, answering her question. Not for weeks.

- Really, she said, pouting, sipping her Chivas on the rocks, he neglects me almost as much as you do - almost.

- Well, he's neglecting me too, said Saburo.

- He's out with Mr. Paul again. What those two find to talk about I just do not know. He's a foreigner after all.

- Who is this Mr. Paul? asked Saburo.

- Some business acquaintance of Hiroshi-san's that we are being nice to. And so, I might add is your little lesbian pal. And it was I who introduced them. So there, ha-ha.

- Have I met him? he wondered.

- How would I know? He's a foreigner.

- American?

- Of course. I'm not referring to a Korean or anything like that, she said with a little laugh. He's a perfectly respectable foreigner.

- Don't know that I ever met him, said Saburo.

- Well, she said, you will, if you come, as I hope you will, to a little party we are giving for him just before he goes back to his native land.

She went into details, time, place, and then wondered if he was seeing anything of Mitsuko.

- Never met the man, wouldn't know.

- No, no. You. Silly.

To which he could honestly answer that he was not.

Further conversation was interrupted by the entrance of another woman. One was most unusual in the Regency; two were unprecedented. The customers stared in consternation, the bartender simply threw up his hands.

The new one was a large blonde in a beaded ball gown, wearing a tiara, carrying a fan. She peered about nearsightedly and then gave a small scream of recognition and tripped over to Saburo.

- Well, imagine that. I just drop in and there you are! Long time no see.

- Madame Mariko, Miss Miki. The latter curtsied but the former barely nodded, then hissed audibly: I thought it said no foreigners allowed.

Saburo dropped his funny little grin but Miss Miki took no offense. It's the operation, she said. My eyes. Makes me look so foreign. See? How lustrous. And she batted her lashes a few times.

Mariko turned away, as though in disgust, and Saburo and Miss Miki continued. She had just wanted to take a peek at the old place before it vanished forever. Her new place was going to be right here - and she pointed at the ceiling - though several stories up of course. She was thinking of calling it the Oberon.

Mariko, listening nonetheless, now turned and pointed: Is that real?

- Oh, no, said Miss Miki, knowing at once what

was meant. She carefully removed the tiara. Then the blonde wig. There she sat, a large, crew-cut, made-up man.

Mariko was surprised. She had perhaps meant only the color of the hair, not the hair itself. The others in the bar, however, were reassured by the disclosure. There were some muffled smiles and many friendly glances.

- Well, said Saburo, always the one to appear unruffled: Oberon seems a pretty good name to me.

- Yes, there are five of us, two in kimono and three not. They do classical. We do modern. And the place is to open very, very late.

- And is I imagine to be very, very expensive, said Saburo with a smile. Miki giggled then rubbed her feet: It's these heels, they're new. The rent is awful, she added, apparently referring to the high prices the Oberon would be forced to charge.

- I too am opening a new place, said Mariko suddenly, perhaps irritated at being left out of the conversation: Or, rather, I am opening my newly renovated premises.

And the two were soon deep into details of interior decoration while Saburo sat idly until, perhaps irritated at being left out of the conversation: Do put that back on. Otherwise it looks odd.

- But it's so hot, and I do sweat so.

- Nonetheless.

The wig sat in Miki's lap like a decapitated head. With a sigh he lifted it up and began adjusting it.

- It's backwards, said Mariko helpfully.

- So it is, said Miki with a giggle. Then: You wouldn't have recognized me a few months ago. In my hard hat. We were putting up the new Scala-za Building. So unfriendly to the nails! And he stretched a hand and gazed reflectively at it.

- How did you ever leave the construction business? Mariko, ever avid, wanted to know.

- Oh, I found this patron.

- Oh, of course, said Mariko as though that explained everything. Then: Speaking of patrons, has our little Mitsuko managed to hook anyone yet?

- How would I know? asked Saburo: She's neglecting me.

Mariko waved a finger: Jealousy, Saburo-san, she said, is a very vulgar emotion. Then she laughed her famous throaty laugh.

- We're both being neglected, he said with his famous little smile.

- So we are, so we are, she cried.

Then Miss Miki, perhaps irritated at being left out of the conversation, turned to the young man at the next stool - stocky, crew-cut - and attempted a few comments about the weather: October already, just imagine, soon be quite cold, real sweater-time.

To which he turned and replied with dignity: I am a homosexual.

- Well, just what do you think I am? demanded Miki, offended. Then, as he flounced back toward Mariko, tiara rattling: Really!

After that they continued talking about the weather - such an unseasonable autumn, going to get quite cold soon the weather person had said, etc.

42

- Seen Mitsuko? asked Saburo pushing away the rolling table.

- Not recently, said Sumire, taking off her sweater.

- She know about us?

- Her? laughed her friend: She's so full of her plans she doesn't notice anything.

- Hiroshi?

- Hiroshi, she said unbuttoning her blouse. Oh, look, a new president.

- Don't know that one, said Saburo taking off his coat.

- Last time it was Grant. I recognized him. He came to our country, did you know that?

- But he's dead, said Saburo, removing his necktie.

- Before he died, explained the girl, removing her blouse.

- Oh, said Saburo, taking off his shirt.

President Coolidge looked down at all of this and Sumire said: Lousy food.

- It always is, he said, unbuttoning his trousers.

- Do we have to eat here? We could eat someplace else and then come here, she said, unzipping her skirt.

- No food, no room, said Saburo, perhaps quoting, attempting to step out of his trousers, tottering, sitting down, removing his shoes.

- I see, she agreed, stepping out of her skirt.

- They're in business, like everyone else, opined Saburo, stepping out of his trousers.

- Business, said Sumire. I wonder what it's like, having your own place.

- Now don't you start, said Saburo, taking off his stockings. One's bad enough.

She giggled and unhooked her bra.

He chuckled in reply and removed his undershirt.

- Still, I don't see why she should be the only

one, she said, stepping out of her panties.

- Jealousy is a very vulgar emotion, said Saburo, stepping out of his shorts. Then. What's this? He had pushed the button on the console and nothing had happened. Where's the bed? he wanted to know.

- Just a minute said the naked girl, moving toward the offending mechanism. She gave it a hard kick with a sturdy foot. There was an apologetic click and the foldout sofa unfolded.

- Thanks, said Saburo, scratching himself.

- Her problem, said Sumire, is that she loses everything by playing hard to get.

She then lowered herself onto the sofa and lay back as though to indicate that she herself did not.

43

- Well, things have certainly changed, was Mitsuko's opinion, looking around, at the band, the wheeling waiters, Tokyo twinkling below: One of them first brought me here. And I met the other one here for the first time.

- Which was which? asked Sumire, quite dressed up and wearing scent.

- Hiroshi-san was the first and Saburo-san was the second. What is that?

- My Sin, answered her friend.

- I thought that was a lipstick.

- My Sin is a whole line, said Sumire, knowledgeably.

- Oh, said Mitsuko and looked out of the window. Then: I just don't know what to do.

- Won't cough up, eh?

- Says the Yamato is such an expense. Really. She's gotten enough out of him if you ask me. All those years. And both of them so old.

- Yes, make way for youth, said Sumire, perhaps quoting.

At this Mitsuko, head to one side, looked quizzically at her dressed-up friend.

- When did you find out? then asked the latter lowering her eyes to her pie.

- Almost at once, said the former: I have these friends now at the Colonial. Called one, got the description. It was obviously you - or, rather, you back then. Mousey, he said, flat heels. I must say I was surprised.

- I was carried away, said Sumire, certainly quoting,

- Oh, that's all right. He's cute but it wouldn't have come to anything.

- That's just what he said.

- See? Then, in a mordant mood: And I only asked you to make a pass at him to make her jealous and now if I am not careful I'll be jealous myself.

- Jealousy, began Sumire, is a very -

- I know, I know, said Mitsuko, waving her hand. Strange, isn't it. Then, laughing: Oh, Mariko will just wet herself -

- All over the new tatami, chortled Sumire.

- The customers will slide in it, giggled Mitsuko.

- And slip and fall down, screamed Sumire.

- No, no, no! cried Mitsuko, helpless, waving her arms.

The headwaiter, dread in every line, hurried to the table. After more laughter and an explanation he retired, shaken but relieved.

- So you had Coolidge? then wondered Mitsuko.

- Oh, is that which one it was?

- Always. Why do these men always choose that president?

- Maybe it's the management. To keep track.

- Fold-out sofa broken?

- Yes, but I fixed it.

- How?

- I kicked it.

Mitsuko looked at her friend with something resembling admiration. Then: Getting so butch we'll have to get you a job at the Kon.

- Wasn't that place something though? asked Sumire, dimpling.

- Yes, but so specialized. It will never reach the general public.

- Still, it must be a real moneymaker.

Mitsuko nodded. Yes, did you see how much poor Saburo had to pay? Adding: Things forbidden cost money.

Sumire, not placing the quote, said: Who said that?

- I did, said Mitsuko. then, sharply: What's that?

- Oh, some old tune, like they do here.

- I never heard them do that, said Mitsuko.

Seeing interest certainly, scenting profit probably, Satch (Happy) Suzuki began to croon along with his Streamliners.

Sumire listened for a bit and then said: A sentimental journey? Now what on earth could that be?

44

- Just like old times, declared Mariko. Just you and me together.

- This place what you have in mind? said Hiroshi looking dubiously at the kneeling youth. Then: Is this what you're going to make Minoru do?

- Something like it, she said. But I think a full obeisance would be more elegant. Just kneeling is a bit casual for the kind of atmosphere I have in mind.

After they had ordered and the youth had shuffled away, Mariko gave her little smile and said: Nevertheless, it is good being out with you again, Hiroshi-san.

- Just how many hundreds of times have we been out? he wondered. How many nights?

- But rarely out so late, she said with a roguish air. Here it is near midnight. Usually I am back at the Yamato just working away, doing my little best. But now since the Yamato is being renovated we have this tiny vacation from our workaday lives. So let's try to have just a bit more fun.

Hiroshi ruefully sipped his Chivas.

-Oh, I know how you feel, she continued. Having to give up Mitsuko like that. And you *were* interested, weren't you. But, just think, at least she's more or less intact except maybe for the Mistress.

- What do you mean now? he asked, perhaps indicating that this subject had been broached before.

- Why, when I heard what that friend of yours,

Saburo Tanaka, had gone and done with that lesbian friend of hers, well, I could scarcely believe it.
And right there, at the Colonial, of all places!

- Your spy?

- My friend! she severely corrected. But, at least I
am thankful for your sake that Mitsuko was not
involved. Think how awful you would have felt if it
had been her instead of that Sumire person. But
think how I must have felt. There he was. Saburo-
san. Behaving like that.

- Would you have preferred that it was me? he
asked, suddenly acute.

Pretty confusion ensued and repeated protesta-
tions that she had no idea of what he was talking
about. Then, upon some silent thought: Let's just
call off the party.

Hiroshi looked at her. I don't see how we can.
Everyone is invited. And Mr. Paul is an important
business acquaintance. He might take it wrong,
might think it was some Japanese plot for all I
know. These foreigners can turn suddenly suspicious, you know.

She nodded, agreeing, but added: Still, he doesn't
seem to have all that good a time with us. I should
think he is probably wanting to be off with his own
kind, don't you think?

- You can never tell. In any event, I think it is better to have the party. Can you face them?

- Who?

- The guilty couple.

- Humph! was the reply, indicating perhaps that the couple meant to her nothing at all. Then, turning back with a roguish smile, she asked: And can you face *her*?

- Who? he asked, already smiling.

- Well, not the guilty party because that is you, you see. So I will simply have to say, the guilty object of your admiration.

- Humph! he said, snapping his fingers and the youth knelt low before him.

- No, no, no, cried Hiroshi: Can't one even have a private conversation around here without all this bowing and scraping?

- Now, now, dear, said Mariko. This is their trademark, their little way of being different here. We mustn't disparage them. We are all in the same business, after all.

- I am not in this business, he said sharply. I am the president of a company. We make things. We sell them. We serve a common need.

- Well, what do you think I do? asked Mariko sharply. If there weren't this common need I wouldn't be in business at all.

He shook his head: It's not the same.

She shook hers: It's identical.

After which they began talking about the party

and how much trouble it was to redo the Yamato (and how expensive, he added) and how they hoped it would go well, and how they thought it might not be too cold that evening - just simple, bracing, autumnal weather.

45

- Interesting little place, said Saburo looking about the darkened street: Should be somewhere around here.

It was late, cold. The two men were alone on the deserted street and a chill wind blew.

- Oh, here it is, said Saburo.

The large, square room, the brick-patterned wallpaper, the black-painted chairs and tables, the candles in bottles were the same but it was now brightly lighted, plastic flowers were stuck into empty straw-covered flasks of Chianti, on the walls posters of sunny Italian climes.

Madame Kon, a rose in her hair, appeared in an apron: Welcome, welcome. *Buon giorno*. Oh, it's you.

- What happened? asked Saburo.

- Well, you know how it is. Times being what they are. And we only had so many customers. And they were always the same. And so, their being so few, we had to keep raising the prices. And so, eventually, they stopped coming. Last one dropped away just last week.

Saburo nodded. He had seen business failures before.

- And so, since we had the candles and the checkered tablecloths anyway, we're an Italian restauraunt now. Didn't you see the sign outside? Capri. That's us.

A waitress in peasant blouse appeared, large scrawled menu in hand. She stopped, looked: Oh. Hi.

- Hello, Miss Aki. You are much changed.

- It's the skirt. Then: You want to eat something? It's no good. I'm the cook.

- Well . . .

- Or, I can meet you when I get off. I still got my boots, though I'm a little out of practice.

She looked more closely, squinted: Hey, you're not Matsuyama-san from Shiseido, are you? No, I guess not. Sorry. I got to get myself some glasses.

- Hope your prices aren't what they were, said Saburo, jocular.

- Oh, no. Different commodity, said Madame Kon quite seriously.

After they were drinking their corked Chianti

alone in the cavernous room and Aki was busy in the kitchen, Hiroshi turned to his friend: Well, how was it? he asked, unfriendly.

- Little Sumire? asked Saburo, acute as always, Very nice. And he held up two fingers, V-for-Victory, to indicate how nice it had been.

- Nicer than Mitsuko? asked Hiroshi surly. I suppose you got into her, too.

Saburo sat back in his chair as though surprised. Mitsuko? he asked as though unable to believe his ears. Mitsuko? No, no, what sort of friend would I be if I did a thing like that? No, not at all. She was yours. Yours from the start. I don't even know why I was bothering to see her.

- I asked you to, said Hiroshi.

- That's right. I'd forgotten. Then: Hey, you asked me to see her and now you're complaining that I went and saw her.

- It's a matter of degree, said Hiroshi.

- Well, you're safe, said his friend, And so is she. Then: You get a look at her friend?

- Just once. Sort of mousey, I thought.

- That's with her clothes on, explained Saburo.

- Oh.

The food was brought. Spaghetti alla Napolitana, sort of. They tried it, then put down their forks. Saburo took a large drink of wine. Hiroshi took a mouthful of water and gargled.

- Enjoy your meal, fellows, said Madame Kon from the corner. I'm busy with dessert.

- Whatever happened to Japanese food? asked Saburo. Remember sushi and sashimi and miso soup and gohan? Almost impossible to make bad gohan. I'd defy even Miss Aki here to do that.

- I don't know, sighed his friend. Too expensive for one thing. Too much trouble for another. Ever tried to make miso soup? You start with dashi, he began -

- I know, I know, interrupted Saburo. Then, looking around: You wouldn't have believed this place when it was going good.

- I suppose you took her here, said Hiroshi, suddenly heavy again.

- Took them both here, said Saburo, as though that made it better.

- They take to the whip? asked Hiroshi. Did they cry and plead like you wanted them to? Did you get really gross? Enemas and things?

- No, no, no, said Saburo. You got it all wrong. That's only in the comic books. Here in real-life Japan, it's different. That beating up girls is just fantasy. You know, masturbation-manual stuff for the man on the street. In real life it's just the opposite. The only S/M parlors are those where the girls beat up the guys.

- Oh. Then you induced those two sweet girls to beat you?

- No, no, no, said Saburo. No one did anything like that at all. We just watched.

- Remembering the good old times, eh? called Madame Kon, busy in the kitchen. Often do myself.

- Are you sure? asked Hiroshi, stabbing his pasta.

- They never beat me up once, honest.

- No, not that. That you never had anything to do with Mitsuko.

- Never touched her. Not once. Not, I must admit, that I would have turned it down had it been offered.

Hiroshi seemed mollified, yet not entirely, for he next said: That was because you were so sated with Mariko, I suppose.

Saburo mimicked helplessness. Look - what are you saying? Madame Mariko is like an old family friend. And she is your friend, Watanabe-kun. Now how could I have done a thing like that. Even if it were possible. Which it wasn't.

- And I sometimes wondered if you weren't a touch homo, admitted Hiroshi, mordant: Running around with the folks you do. And now look at you. You've gone and had all three of them for all I know!

Saburo raised both hands in a gesture of defeat. Look, Old Classmate, you just ask them - any of them. They'll tell you that nothing happened. Then, with a smile: At least not with two of them. But the third one, little Sumire, she might tell you something different.

This appeal brought a grudging smile and Hiroshi contented himself with: Well, you'll be seeing your harem again at the party at the end of the month.

Saburo began his boyish grin, then looked with surprise and repulsion at what Madame Aki had set before them.

- What is that?
- Zabaglione, Italian! Made it myself.
- What's in it?
- Eggs, sugar, cream. Supposed to be marsala only we didn't have any so I used sake.

Saburo looked at the glass. I can see the eggs, he said. They're scrambled.

Hiroshi gazed. So they are, he said.

Madame Kon peered, then stared at the cookbook lying open on the bar, and then - very much her old self - said: Shit!

46

Tokyo twinkled. The waiters waited in the gloom. It was late. Even the Streamliners and their genial leader appeared impatient. And still the table of three - talking, laughing - remained.

- Don't care if I ever go home, said Mariko throwing back her head. This has been just lovely, Mr. Paul. She then looked around and held up her wine glass, empty.

- It's past midnight, though, said Hiroshi, staring down at the avenues bright with the headlights of those, it seemed, returning home.

- And cold, said Paul pleasantly.

The headwaiter approached, sighed, received his order.

- You didn't order a whole bottle, did you? asked Hiroshi.

- No, just a glass. Starlight Lounge is very modern. Serves by the glass. Oh, do look at it, the dear Starlight Lounge, she said indicating the glowering waiters, the frowning band: It never changes.

- Unlike everything else, she continued, perhaps thinking of the Yamato, or of life itself. Then, remembering her host: And another change is that in a few weeks you will be gone, all gone . . .

And Mariko, now in a pensive mood, ran a reflective finger down her empty glass.

- Where are they all going? she wondered, gazing down at the traffic: Biggest city in the world, everyone going someplace all the time. Why don't they just stop?

The wine appeared. Hiroshi looked at it as though disapproving. Mariko, his expression seemed to say, had had enough.

- Hiroshi-san, she said. Why don't they stop? They should. Don't you ever feel that something awful is going to happen? I mean like terrible.

- An earthquake? asked Paul, helpfully.

- No, worse. Like some enormous explosion, like it's all been wound up too tight, like it's going to explode.

- Well, my dear, began Hiroshi, common sense itself, I don't really see that -

- No, no, no, she cried, inspired by her vision. Like a time bomb. Like a volcano. I am a seer. I can see the future.

The headwaiter appeared, hovered.

- It's just modern life, said Mr. Paul judiciously.

- It's closing time, said the headwaiter.

This they found funny. Mariko shrieked, Paul giggled, Hiroshi chuckled and the headwaiter retreated.

- Oh, how amusing, she cried, wiping her eyes, apocalyptic thoughts now fled.

Then: Well, he's right, of course. This has been a most pleasant evening, my dear Mr. Paul, and I thank you very much for it. We will be making our small return, as you know, at this modest little gathering we are giving you at the new Yamato at the end of the month. She then belched and smiled at everyone in sight.

- Did you really go? See the Mistress? her host suddenly asked.

- What? asked Mariko, whose ability to see the future had not prepared her for this question.

- No, I wondered. I am going home. I wanted to know. How things turned out.

She looked at him, then giggled and said: Well, since things have turned out so well I can tell you that I never did. I do not even know the Mistress. We have never met. My threat, however, was just one of the many weapons in my arsenal. And here she looked in a roguish manner at Hiroshi.

- I see. Thank you, said Mr. Paul.

- Not at all, she answered graciously, then to Hiroshi: Didn't know that, did you? Well, it was for your sake that I was guilty of that little white lie, my dear. I saw no other way to save you from the wiles of that person. I had to frighten her into decency, you see. Hence my little subterfuge.

- Not only for me, said Hiroshi with a certain dignity.

- That is true, she said, more dignified still. It was for your friend. To save him from a similar fate. Because he was your classmate. I am capable, you see, of that kind of sacrifice. In this way, I was able to save you both.

Hiroshi turned a weary glance toward Mr. Paul who blinked and said: Mitsuko was worried.

- Such was the intention, said Mariko with a quiet grace. Then added: I thought it better such, just a little quiet thought on my part, no jealous scenes, jealousy after all is so common.

Hiroshi sighed and looked at Tokyo, cold, asleep.

The headwaiter hovered.

- Yes, we ought to leave, I suppose, said Mariko as Mr. Paul, producing one of several small plastic cards, began signing.

- Heavens, it is so late. I never notice the time at the Yamato but now that I am on vacation while it is being redone I have turned into a regular clock-watcher.

- Speaking of which, Watanabe-san, she continued: I am thinking of installing time clocks at the place now. The girls are terrible, sneaking in late or out early. This way I can keep track. What do you think of that?

- Anything you say, dear, said Hiroshi, quiet this evening.

- Oh, dear, you have gone and paid, she cried, as though just now noticing. Really, Mr. Paul. You shouldn't have. It was so delicious. I just love their chicken à la king here.

And she twinkled, swayed, was supported by both, then twinkled again, and finally, carefully began to find her way through the waiters and the gloom.

Half way to the doors of the Starlight Lounge, she stopped, looked about her, as though she had forgotten something, then focused her eyes on the empty bandstand. Satch (Happy) Suzuki and his Streamliners were gone. It was as though they had never been.

47

Late. Cold wind. Winter coming. Hiroshi drunk.

- My problem is - , he began.

- Your problem is that you're not doing anything you really want to. Good job, wife, kids, something on the side, and it isn't enough.

The Businessman's Bar and Lounge, all anonymous hi-tech in far Ikebukuro, with capsules for those who missed the last train.

Hiroshi looked up at the old barman - reddish hair, blueish eyes.

- You half? wondered Hiroshi, squinting.

- Mother's Japanese, said the barman civilly. Father's not.

- Occupation baby, said Hiroshi, closing one eye, focusing.

- You might say that, said the man.

- How come you know so much about me?

- It's not just you. That description fits everyone who comes in.

- I remember back then, said Hiroshi.

- Me too, said the barman.

- Have a drink, said Hiroshi suddenly.

- Don't mind if I do.

- That's when our country changed, said Hiroshi.

- One of the times, said the barman, sipping.

- When was another?

- Meiji Restoration, the Olympics, you name it.

- Change, change, said Hiroshi, as though sadly. Then: Couldn't you get any other kind of job than this? No, I guess not. Not looking like that.

- I'm lucky. Most men like me, unless they're good-looking, end digging up the streets. If they're good-looking they get to be models. For a while. Girls got it better. They get to be singers or dancers if they're lucky. Prostitutes if they're not.

- That's because you look different from us, said Hiroshi. And we are a homogeneous nation, he added, quoting.

- We're not all that homogeneous if we've got me, said the man

- No. You are the exception, said Hiroshi. Can you speak English or anything?

- No. Just Japanese, like you.

- But can you read or write? I know this white man and he can talk but he can't read or write.

The barman held up a book.

- What's that?

- Japanese.

- I can see that much.

- I read a lot. The place is usually empty at this hour.

- When was it I last read a book? asked Hiroshi, as though in wonder. Then, as though in answer: *Miyamoto Musashi.* When I was young. It's about this swordsman. I liked it, my, but I liked it. Then: That's the real Japanese tradition.

- Yes, I'm afraid so, agreed the bartender, book on bar.

- What's yours?

- Nagai Kafu.

- Who that? Wait. I remember something. No, it's gone.

- He's a Japanese writer.

- I could tell that from the name.

- He would have hated Tokyo now, said the barman looking at the etched glass, the steel tables, the gray enameled walls, the chrome corners. But then he hated it then.

- How could anyone hate Tokyo? asked Hiroshi, seriously.

- He only hated Tokyo as it was then, but he

loved it as it had been, before he was in it.

- Funny, said Hiroshi. Sounds like a regular trouble-maker to me. Not a part of the Japanese tradition at all.

- He really loved it, was the barman's opinion: But he believed that things naturally got worse as time went on.

- That's an original thought, said Hiroshi looking around the cold room: We're taught to believe that things get better.

- Yes, agreed the barman, also looking around. That's what we're taught.

- And I believe it, said Hiroshi. Why, if things didn't get better, then nothing would be worthwhile, would it now?

- No, it wouldn't, said the barman with a smile.

- There, you see? said Hiroshi. This man that you're reading. He sounds like he never had any fun.

The barman looked at Hiroshi.

- I like a novel to be familiar, said Hiroshi.

- You like everything to be familiar, said the barman.

- Hey, so I do, said Hiroshi, blinking: How did you know that? You magic or something? Drink up. Then: Who wants to be original anyway? We always get criticized, we Japanese, for being copiers. Well, why not, I say, why not? The familiar is the best.

- I think everyone copies, said the intellectual

barman, sipping: Nothing is original - ever. Things seem to be changing but they are always the same.

- Like Tokyo, said Hiroshi.

- We dote on the new, not sensing the old, said the philosophical barman.

- Doting, said Hiroshi, pensive.

- A quality evergreen, said the barman, perhaps quoting.

- Really?

- And so does everyone - copy. Perhaps it's that we Japanese hide it less.

- Hey, said Hiroshi, you said we Japanese.

- So I did.

Silence. Then: But what about love? Hiroshi wanted to know, face in fist.

- Love isn't original at all, said the barman.

- I don't mean that. I mean what about love? What's supposed to be so good about it? Why is everyone all upset over it? Why are all the novels about it?

- I should think that business would be enough, he continued, but it isn't. And not the family either, though I've got one. And I got this girl. Well, she's a woman now, and I been putting up the money for her place for years now, and I guess it must be love, but . . .

And so Hiroshi went on and had the kind of talk one usually has with barmen and after a while he fell off the stool and the barman picked him up, as they do.

Then the man with the reddish hair and the blueish eyes took off his customer's shoes, loosened his tie and his belt and put him into a capsule.

It was a long metal tube with a steel-and-glass door like a washing machine. Inside was a narrow pallet and at the far end, to be viewed between the feet, if one was conscious, a television set. There was also a humidifier, a filter, and an air-conditioning unit. Also a No Smoking sign. It was like a spaceship sleeping-unit, as glimpsed in the films, or like some hi-tech coffin. Here Hiroshi spent a quiet night.

48

- Welcome, welcome, moaned Minoru, nose to the new tatami.

- What's the matter with him? asked Hiroshi, carefully stepping over the kimonoed, prostrate form.

- Allergy, he says, said Mariko. But in October? Maybe it's the tatami. It's after midnight. He's been at it for hours.

Then, to Mr. Paul, indicating the sniffling, wheezing young man on the floor: Very Japanese.

And to the rest of the party, Mitsuko, Sumire, Saburo: Well, here we are - the New Yamato.

The genkan of the New Yamato held, beside Minoru, a very large folding screen by a very minor master, and behind it a refrigerator for which there was no room in the kitchen. Beside it, sitting on its lacquered box, was a set of real samurai armor, horned helmet and all, the face mask, hanging beneath, appearing surprised to find itself in such surroundings.

Then, past the fusuma, was the large tatami-floored club itself holding many low tables and zabuton cushions, andon lamps, wired, shoji panels set into the walls, electric bulbs behind, shelf on shelf of Johnny Walker Black, four golf trophies and two stuffed fish.

Everyone looked. Mariko again turned to Mr. Paul. Very Japanese, she said. Then: Make yourself at home.

This was something which others of the guests seemed to be having difficulty in doing. Some were sitting on the floor, massaging their feet. A few were standing, rubbing their knees. Several of the girls, a whole evening of kneeling behind them, were now sitting on the tables, obi slipped, kimono gaping,

- Just takes some getting used to, said Mariko indicating their table and its six zabuton. After all, our ancestors suffered. Why shouldn't we?

- Nice crowd, said Saburo, lowering himself to the floor.

- Payday, Mariko explained.

- Wonderful, said Mr. Paul, who actually seemed to be admiring the effect.

- I don't know if I can manage this, said Sumire, giggling, confused: My skirt might ride up.

- We've thought of everything, said Mariko with a motherly smile. She clapped her hands and Emiko appeared with a large doily.

- Here, said Mariko. You just put this in your lap, you see, and then it doesn't matter how far your skirt rides up. You want one, dear? This to Mitsuko.

- No, thank you, was the reply.

- This is going to ruin the crease in my pants, said Hiroshi with a smile.

- Well, I'd think you'd put up with a little for the sake of the atmosphere. And Saburo-san here, so polite, hunkering right down without a word of complaint.

- It's difficult to sit like this with your shoes on, mildly countered Hiroshi.

- Yes, agreed Mariko, nodding. That's so. But on the other hand - first, if you made them take off their shoes no one would come, and, second, you'd have deprived them of the novel pleasure of dancing on tatami shod.

As she said this Midori was putting on *Werner Müller Plays Japanese Melodies for Dancing*, and to the strains of 'Sakura, Sakura' done as a fox trot, several of the guests stood up, grasped their hostesses and began sliding about with their shoes on.

- There, isn't that nice?

- Well, said Hiroshi, it is certainly novel.

- Folks seem to be enjoying it, said Saburo with his little smile: Maybe you got yourself a good idea here.

Mariko dimpled and Emiko appeared with sushi, tofu, jellyfish, sea slug, squid, octopus and Kraft on Ritz.

I can't tell you how much this cost, giggled Mariko. Things Japanese are so expensive now.

- The kimono alone, said Sumire politely, looking around.

- Are you telling me! was the gracious rejoinder. The money! Eh, Hiroshi? The kimono are all used, of course. Used just once though. At weddings. That's why they're so bright and have birds and things on them. But they do add a spot of color, don't they now?

- Oh, yes, indeed, said Sumire, honestly.

- We only need now our fair hostess in a kimono, our daughter of Old Japan, said Saburo gallantly.

- Me? and Mariko slapped the air with pleasure. Oh, I'm too old for kimono as bright as that Then, seriously: And anything sober wouldn't let me stand out, you see. As is fitting.

- Well, it's just lovely, whatever it is, said Mitsuko, referring to her hostess's ensemble.

- Hanae Mori, said Mariko with simplicity. Butterflies. She suits women like me.

There was a short silence after this, interrupted by the sudden extinguishing of the illumination, the plangent strains of Werner Müller's koto, and a baby spot. The floor show had began.

A young person in a purple kimono appeared carrying a fan in one hand and some paper wisteria blossoms in the other. She made a few tentative movements.

Hiroshi turned to Mr. Paul: Nice little girl. Talented. From Saitama. Went to school especially to learn.

Mr. Paul smiled appreciatively, then looked again: I've seen her somewhere before, he said.

Hiroshi nodded, pleased: She's famous.

Duty over, the girl bobbed and exited into the kitchen, dragging her wisteria. Werner Müller was then shoved aside by Shep Fields and his Rippling Rhythm. Time to dance. Several stood. Paired.

- Did you see that? Mariko wanted to know, shuffling about on the tatami in the arms of Hiroshi:

She snapped him right up, just like that. And I thought she was supposed to be mousey. Pretty forward mouse!

- Wanted him for yourself, didn't you? You looked right at him, you know.

- Watanabe-san, I will tolerate no jealousy. I think that jealousy is -

- All right, all right, all right.

Nearby, Sumire was saying in an injured tone: I've been waiting for you to call,

- Busy, busy. Work, work, said Saburo, easily.

- Well, I just hope you aren't the kind who kiss and run, she said.

- Better than being the kind who kiss and tell, he countered.

Left at the table, Mitsuko said: My feet are falling asleep.

- I'm falling asleep all over, said Mr. Paul. It's after midnight.

He then straightened up and looked around: It really looks like Japan, doesn't it?

- Yes - in a way, was her opinion.

- It is different from the last time we were here.

- Yes, she said. How long ago that seems. Way last spring. And I was supposed to be your date.

He nodded at the memory, then looking at the dancers he asked who this Saburo was.

At that point Shep Fields stopped and those

dancing returned to the table to sip and bite and chat until he started up again.

Once Saburo had partnered Mariko across the tatami in her spike heels, she said: I've been waiting for you to call.

His arm around her, he said: Busy, busy. Work, work.

- I think you have forgotten all about me. Heartless.

In another portion of the dance floor, Mitsuko said: I've been waiting for you to call

- Look, said Hiroshi. What with Mariko and redoing this place, not to mention my own job, and my own wife, who's gotten a little difficult recently for some reason, I just haven't had the time. Then: Besides, you've got Saburo-san haven't you?

- Not anymore, she said, looking across the room.

At the table Sumire, holding tightly onto her doily, was volunteering: This is my first time here.

- It is my last, said Mr. Paul. I leave tomorrow.

- Back to your native land, divined the girl, then: Oh, to see a foreign land, with my own eyes!

Mr. Paul smiled understandingly and asked who this Saburo person was - Hiroshi's old classmate? Didn't really look old enough.

The rippling rhythms ceased and the four returned to the two left behind. Then there was more eating and drinking until, yet once more, the familiar sound of someone blowing through a straw into a glass of water was heard.

- I've been waiting for you to call, said Mitsuko in an injured tone

- Who is that foreigner? asked Saburo, as though in answer.

- Funny. He asked about you too.

- Not funny at all, two men meeting for the first time. Didn't even exchange cards.

- Well, he's very nice. And he speaks - talks and everything but no reading and writing, I think.

- I'd imagine not, said Saburo as though gauging this difficulty.

- And he just loves things Japanese. See how proper he has been sitting all evening though it must be killing him, those long legs and all. He likes tansu, things like that. He really understands us, says Hiroshi-san.

Then, as though trying again: I've been waiting for you to call.

In another part of the dance floor Sumire, with a captivating simper, blinking her little eyes, said: Mitsuko-san has told me so very much about you.

- Not too much I hope, said Hiroshi with a little shake of the head.

- Oh, no. Just what a very kind and understanding person you are. I admire that in a man. Very much. Every woman wants, needs, someone kind and understanding, I do think.

Hiroshi held her closer and they stepped about the room.

- Oops, sorry, he said, having stepped on her foot.

- Oh, no. My fault, she gasped.

Meanwhile, at the table: Thinking? asked Mr. Paul looking at Mariko, pensive.

She patted his hand: Just thinking of the old times. We had this monkey.

- Yes. I heard.

- Died. Poor thing. Used to play in the plastic ivy, poor thing. Then rousing herself: Don't you ever dance?

- My legs fell asleep, he answered.

- Oh, well, I can understand that. Then: Look at them, and she indicated her other patrons. Half of them can't stand up at all. Might be good for business. Can't get up to go home. Ha-ha.

Her merriment was short-lived. Soon she was looking at the dancing couples. Little viper, she said.

- Mitsuko-san?

- No, no. The mousey one, the one who calls herself Sumire.

- She seems to be getting on well with Hiroshi.

- Just as though she hadn't already made off with Saburo-san. Really, the young people these days!

Then: Poor Mitsuko-san. She's a good girl, really. Just badly confused. Well, I hope she goes back to the Mistress like a good girl ought now that this false friend of hers, this Sumire person, has apparently decided to go straight.

- Oh, I don't think either of the girls are . . .

- Where there's smoke there's fire, said Mariko darkly: I'm trying to find out where this Sumire works right now. I have my people busy on it. I will go and see her employer and complain about this.

Everyone returned at the table, Shep Fields off, Werner Müller back on, more eating and drinking, then Mariko struggled to her feet, pulled at her Hanae Mori and raised a glass.

- I want to drink to the men in my life, she cried: Here's to them. Here is to Mr. Paul, whose party this is, who is returning, fittingly, to his native land tomorrow. And here is to Tanaka-san. He was once a true friend indeed and I hope that perhaps he may be once more in the future.

Then she gave her famous throaty laugh. And here is to my very own Hiroshi-san, my oldest friend among the three, and the one who is paying the bill tonight. Whee! she cried, waving her full glass about.

- Wa! cried Hiroshi, drenched, and then began sponging up with the first thing to hand.

- Yah! cried Sumire, trying to hold down her skirt with one hand while grabbing for the doily with the other.

- Oh, sorry, said Hiroshi, returning it

- Oh, it's all wet, she cried.

- Midori, Midori, called Mariko, perhaps intending to order another doily.

Emiko hobbled out and whispered in her ear.

- Really! said Mariko. Midori's obi has come off and she can't get it tied again.

At which she stood, then collapsed. My feet, she cried. They've gone to sleep.

After much rubbing by Hiroshi and expressions of sympathy from a solicitous Mitsuko, she stood and then, exhibiting a game limp, went to assist the clutching Midori.

- Some people in their relation with one another, said someone, are always doing similar things but never for similar reasons.

- Who said that? asked someone else, but there was no answer.

And so it went. More food, more drink, more merriment, some wonderment and a few quotations, while it grew later than any of them thought and far overhead the moon sailed and sank.

When Hiroshi consulted his wrist he was surprised.

- Five? he asked, shocked. It must have stopped. He shook it. Seiko though, he added, as if in wonderment.

- Three, said Mariko, her head on his shoulder. Three men, three women. You would think that would mean one for each. But no, oh, no. Then, near tears: Oh, Hiroshi-san, why is life so difficult?

- Love, he said. Love is hard.

Saburo, who had been deep in conversation with Paul, looked up, gave his little smile and said: Well, I never heard that love was soft.

Sumire slapped at him. Oh, you, she said and yawned, then returned to her talk with Mitsuko.

Mr. Paul listened to his new friend, dragging his thumb through the natto while Saburo fingered a sushi.

Mitsuko looked into her glass and then tried to pick out the ice cubes while Sumire, confiding it would seem, talked on, chewing a sea slug the while. And Hiroshi, eyes closed, almost asleep, settled slowly under the weight of Mariko.

Time passed.

Emiko approached. Mariko, startled, opened her eyes and looked around.

The six were alone - but for hobbling Emiko, blinking Midori, and Minoru, wheezing and watering in the kitchen and wanting to go home.

- Well, we've made a night of it, it seems, said Mariko, yawning, stretching, then turning to look at Hiroshi as though with new eyes.

- Hello, you, she said playfully, pushing his nose with one finger. Then, as though surprised: You know, you're not so bad after all.

The others were also now rousing themselves.

- Will you look at the time, said Saburo. You sure know how to give a party, he added with his irritating little smile. Well, time to hit the hay, he said, then turned to Paul: How about you, fella?

- Yes, I have this plane to catch.

- That's tomorrow.

- No, tomorrow's today now.

- But that's only in the afternoon, right? Mariko-san, Hiroshi-san, thanks for a great party, and I'll just take the guest of honor off your hands for you. He's really something. Why, he understands us Japanese even better than we understand ourselves. Then, lowering his voice: He's had a little too much to drink, maybe. But I'll see him back to the hotel. I'll do that much for you.

- I've had too much to drink, said Paul, perfectly sober.

All three women showed their surprise and, to a certain extent, their disappointment.

- Bye-bye now, see you later, Saburo was saying, shaking the hands of the two younger, kissing that of the elder. Then the two men were across the tatami, up the stairs and out.

- Well, said Sumire.

Mariko looked over at her, smiled, said nothing. Mitsuko began smoothing her dress preparatory, it would seem, to leaving.

- I just don't know what to think, pursued Sumire.

- I know, said Mitsuko, and added yet another quote: Life's like that.

Then the two young ladies were on their feet, assuring their hostess of what a good time indeed they had had and apologizing for the lateness of the hour. And with several long, apparently last looks at Hiroshi, they were up the stairs.

- You are the only one left out, my dear, said Mariko.

- What?

- You are the only one of our number whom your friend didn't take out.

- What? he repeated, sleepy. Then: Wouldn't have been right, we're fellow classmates.

- To each his own, said Mariko wisely: That is best.

- What do you mean? asked Hiroshi straightening up to look at the mess on the table, at the littered tatami.

- I mean you and me, Hiroshi, dear. I've been thinking about it - us. Now I know that you have had this roving eye. No, no, no, not a word. I was about to admit that it is natural for you to have had one. Not that I approve, you understand, simply that I understand. But now that is all over, I do believe. We do fit, don't you think?

And there they stood, looking at each other, while the samurai stared and upstairs, past the golf trophies and the minor master, past the ancient kamban, Tokyo stirred.

Bong went the clock on the empty Ginza. Six in the morning, autumn, and the sun just coming up.

Donald Richie is best known as the foremost Western authority on Japanese cinema - his latest work is *A Hundred Years of Japanese Film*. He has also written about many other aspects of the country and its people. His books include *The Inland Sea* and *Public People, Private People*.

David Cozy is a writer and critic living in Chigasaki, Japan. He enjoys writing on authors who are too little known and has published essays about Edward Whittemore, Avram Davidson and Edward Gorey. He is at present writing an overview of the fiction of Guy Davenport.

Isaac Diggs is a photographer based in New York City. His work has been exhibited internationally and is held in private and public collections. The images in *Tokyo Nights* were made during a ten-week residency in Japan supported by the Asian Cultural Council.